Mountainfell

KATHARINE ORTON

WALKER
BOOKS

First published 2022 by Walker Books Ltd
87 Vauxhall Walk, London SE11 5HJ

2 4 6 8 10 9 7 5 3 1

Text © 2022 Katharine Orton
Cover artwork © 2022 Sandra Dieckmann

The right of Katharine Orton to be identified as author
of this work has been asserted in accordance with
the Copyright, Designs and Patents Act 1988

This book has been typeset in Sabon and Tisdall

Printed and bound by CPI Group (UK) Ltd, Croydon CR0 4YY

British Library Cataloguing in Publication Data:
a catalogue record for this book is available from the British Library

ISBN 978-1-5295-0329-6

www.walker.co.uk

This book is for anyone who has ever felt different.
Let's be different together.

Mountainfell

AT FIRST, THE TREMOR FROM THE MOUNTAIN WAS too slight to notice. The villagers of Lofotby, caught between the coast and the dark towering mass of Mountainfell, slumbered on. The rumblings barely invaded their dreams. But the gentle tremor soon became a shake. The shake became a quake.

The final, violent shudder came with a thunderous crack. It lasted only seconds, but it was enough. Throughout the village, eyelids snapped open and hands groped in the darkness for their bedside lamps. Babies cried, and children buried their heads under blankets.

In her home, at the very foot of the mountain, Erskin gripped her sheets until the final rumbles subsided. Nothing like this had ever happened before. For a long time afterwards, she lay awake and listened to the cries of the strange creatures living on the slopes above, knowing that few others would be close enough to hear the eerie yaps, snarls and squawks. She'd heard the odd cry or shriek before, but nothing quite like this – so many, all together.

Though her father always told her not to dwell on such things, it was hard not to wonder what sorts of monsters could make those sounds. Lying there in the darkness, with her heart in her mouth, it felt to Erskin like they may never be silent again.

I

IN THE TWILIGHT HOURS AFTER THE TREMOR, AN anxious crowd gathered in the market square. To Erskin, it seemed like the air coursed with the same dread she'd woken up with as she and her sister moved closer to the dimly lit throng. They, like the others, had come for answers from the Lordsson. What had made the mountain shake? What did it mean for the village?

And then there was the other question that burned in her mind. The most unthinkable question of all. The one that made her blood run icy cold.

Would Lofotby, their village, be attacked? Would those terrible creatures come down from the mountain?

Erskin risked a glance at the looming, misty form of Mountainfell. Towering above this small coastal village that people only ever came to or left by sea, it was a formidable barrier between them and anything else. A nightmarish place, where even the trees were said to conspire to make sure you never came back. And yet, the people of Lofotby were tough. They refused to be driven out by fear of a mountain. They had made this place their home.

The legend was that when their ancestors had first crossed it looking for a new land all those years ago, many had been lost to its terrors. There was talk of witches, beasts with long teeth and even sharper claws – and of course, the dragon. Since then, none of the few who had stepped onto the mountain had ever returned. Not that many of them did so by choice. Every year one – sometimes two – people were chosen by the Lordsson to leave their families behind and go to Mountainfell for good. It was to appease the dragon, and make sure that the village was left in peace. Erskin knew, just as everyone did, that it was necessary for the village's safety – though she hated to see the pain it caused, and lived in dread that it would one day be a member of her family. No one knew for sure if they were dead. But not one of them had ever come back, either.

Erskin's pulse quickened as she glanced up at the wall on which the names of the missing were listed: Alrick, Ragna, Jakob... The list was long –

and it wasn't just villagers. Recently a whole team of scientists came from the mainland, wanting to do research on the mountain. They wouldn't listen to sense, and had never been seen again. At least that year, no one else had to be sent from the village.

Among the carved names was Sibella Sifsdotter's, and it caught Erskin's eye, just as it always did. Aleksander the Lordsson's own sweetheart, who had disappeared on the mountain after it was discovered she was a hex-addled witch – proof that the rumours about her were true. It had been a huge scandal at the time, and Aleksander had never been the same since, but Erskin had been too young to remember. Still, it sent a shiver through her.

She pushed her hand under the lid of the satchel that was slung over one shoulder. Inside, she felt fur of impossible softness, the nuzzle of a gentle nose, then the soothing rub of a whiskered cheek. The telltale vibration as the warm body within began to purr.

Shh. Back to sleep, Scrattletak, Erskin thought, smiling to herself. She was now much calmer. *Stay hidden and safe, you big fluffball.*

As if in response, the cheek stopped its rubbing, and the weight of the body inside the satchel shifted as it readjusted itself to the most comfy spot. Erskin glanced at her elder sister, Birgit, but luckily Birgit was scouring the crowd with her glow lamp held high, and hadn't seen the satchel move of its own accord. Erskin had kept Scrat hidden ever since she'd found him as a tiny, starving kitten by the great wall. Her sister would be furious if she knew Erskin had taken the cat in. People didn't keep pets in Lofotby – only farm animals, strictly for food, clothing, or pest control. And besides, even Erskin had to admit there was something unusual about Scrat. He was quite ... odd-looking. But she loved him anyway.

He always seemed to know what she was thinking, and she him. He was her best, and her only, friend. But the villagers didn't need any more convincing that they, the Mountain Keeper's daughters, weren't normal. Erskin keeping a cat as a pet and carrying it around in a satchel would surely make things worse, if they found out.

Guilt at the thought of how Birgit would react if she knew made Erskin cringe. It felt like every tiny thing she did embarrassed her sister, so something like *this* might finish her off. But Erskin needed Scrat with her for courage – for comfort. No one else had to know. Besides, if she and her sister could just keep their heads down and bring any news straight back to Mam and Dad at the cottage as they'd been asked, all would be well.

Squinting to see better in the gloom, Erskin scanned the crowd absently, until she caught sight of a boy from school. She froze – he was looking right at her. Leif or something, he was called. He was Mara Azidi's son from the market, and in the year below her. They'd never spoken, but this wasn't the first time she'd caught him looking at her. Probably he'd laugh at her later with his friends, like all the others did, although she couldn't remember him ever shouting names at her. He smiled at her now, but she looked away quickly. She didn't want any trouble.

"Erskin!"

Erskin jumped at the annoyance in her sister's voice. "Pay attention for once, will you?" Birgit snapped, dazzling her with the glow lamp. "Stop daydreaming."

A wave of shame rolled over her because Birgit was right: she hadn't been paying attention. Erskin tried not to daydream. She tried really hard. But trying isn't the same as succeeding. Sometimes she focused so much on the *idea* of paying attention, that she forgot to actually do it. Still, she couldn't help a quick glance back to where she'd caught sight of Leif, watching her – but the bustle of bodies had now shifted, and he was gone.

Together, Erskin and Birgit skirted the edge of the crowd in search of a decent view of the man on the platform: Aleksander, the Lordsson. Gold glinted from the embroidery on his lapels as he addressed the gathering. Aleksander was always well dressed, and always wore the golden pin which bore his family crest: two joined spirals that twisted in opposite directions. Erskin didn't know anyone else who had such a thing, but it was obvious how much his family's position meant to him by the way he always showed off the pin. Their bloodline had governed Lofotby, and overseen the offerings, for generations, and Aleksander clearly couldn't wait to be Lord himself. But although Aleksander's father, the Lord of Lofotby, was much older these days, it seemed to Erskin he only ever gave Aleksander the pettiest or worst jobs to do – like addressing a frightened crowd of farmers in the gloom before dayspring.

Erskin looked around. It was still dark enough for the two crescent moons to be visible, and the sprawling web of multicoloured fey-lights were lit. Later today Erskin knew that the warm, sugary smells of the traditional pastries and sweet treats made here would carry all the way to their cottage on the cold, salty air from the sea. Erskin's mouth watered to think of those – but she snapped herself out of it. She'd almost drifted off in a daydream again.

"... here to reassure you that everything is being done to keep our village safe," the Lordsson was saying. "The wall is stronger than ever thanks to the improvements I've put in place. Understand this. We are now safer from the mountain and its dangerous magic than we've been since our ancestors built the wall over two centuries ago. Safer than we've *ever* been, in fact."

"What was that tremor then?" someone from the crowd called out.

"Could it be a sign that the dragon is on the move?" another shouted. "Looking for victims to carry back to the summit? They say its nest is littered with bones..."

Aleksander raised his hands. "No one has seen the cloud dragon in generations," he boomed. "Our offerings keep it happy, and so it doesn't attack. The tremor was likely just a natural phenomenon," he added. "An earthquake. A one-off event."

Erskin shuddered. The Lordsson called the people who were sent to the mountain "offerings", but everyone knew what they really were: sacrifices. The bones littering the dragon's nest were probably theirs.

"There's nothing natural about that mountain," someone called out.

"They say the cloud dragon breathes fire and eats people whole," someone else hissed.

"And it has teeth like needles."

"And claws as sharp as scythes."

The panic was growing.

"Now, now," Aleksander said. "Let's all calm down."

"What if the offerings aren't enough? What if it's run out of food up there and is coming down for us?"

"For our children!"

At this came a sudden hush, and even Aleksander the Lordsson's face fell for a moment. He paused, and his hand went to the golden crest pinned to his lapel, as if for reassurance. Then he seemed to take a deep breath.

"Friends," he said, picking through his words. "The wall is strong."

"But dragons fly!"

Aleksander coughed. "The dragon has never come to the village. We are safe as long as we stay here and keep sending offerings; it will not venture into our territory and the wall will hold back the other creatures."

"How do you know?" came the same swift voice.

The reply was so quick it seemed to catch Aleksander off guard. The crowd grew so quiet that everyone might well have been holding their breath. Erskin definitely was.

A chill wind blew across the square, as icy as saltwater depths. It made the fey-lights shake and clank in the waiting silence. Erskin feared that at any minute the lights might shatter, showering them all with shards of glass. A flurry of donderline seeds carried on pale feathery wisps shaped like tiny umbrellas whipped across the square. *Tell the seeds who is on your mind before you blow on them*, their mam had once told her and Birgit. *And they will go to the one you're thinking of. So, if you're lucky enough to catch a donderline seed, it could mean someone is missing you, too.* Erskin reached out for one, but it twirled away out of her grasp. Flicking a seed off his shoulder, Aleksander cleared his throat.

"Our people have been safe here for over two hundred years. The wall has not failed us yet, and as is our tradition the current Mountain Keeper watches for danger, night and day. If he'd seen any trace of a threat, or any sign that..." He hesitated. "Any sign that the cloud dragon was on the move, he would have raised the alarm. That's what the warning bell is for, after all."

The crowd erupted into whispers and mumbles. Erskin felt the air turn instantly sharp. This would have been a great time to use her ability to "switch off her ears", as her family called it – but that only seemed to work when she didn't mean it to. Before she could help it, the whispers slithered in.

"The Mountain Keeper – that outer-edge dweller..."

"His whole family is hex-addled from living up at that cottage, if you ask me. It's too close to Mountainfell. Dangerous to be so near to all that magic. All that evil..."

"Can he even be trusted to ring the bell, if there's an attack? He's not as young as he was."

"Look, there are his daughters."

"Something's not quite right with them, especially the younger one..."

"Who would want to raise their kids next to that...?"

A flurry of people swivelled to stare at Erskin and Birgit. Suddenly, they were the centre of attention in an ever-growing mob. Erskin's gut twisted. She wanted to hide and she wanted to be sick – but preferably to hide first.

The fey-lights started to clank again, though Erskin could feel no wind this time. Birgit, her face even paler and harder than ever, whipped round. "We've heard enough. Let's go," she growled, and grabbed Erskin roughly by the arm as if it was all somehow *her* fault. Erskin was about to cry out, to protest, but a strange noise stopped them both. It seemed to come from Erskin's stomach.

She looked down at herself, instantly frightened that she really was going to vomit, but the noise hadn't come from her... It had come from her satchel. The satchel which now wriggled and writhed, and mewled again: a sound so eerie and jarring that the people watching gasped, and even Birgit staggered back in fright.

Oh, no, Erskin thought, panic rising in her throat. Scrat.

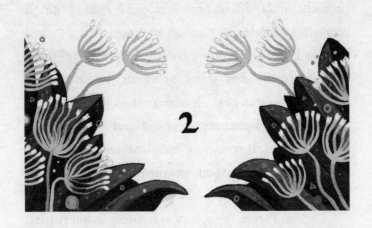

2

Erskin reached down to pull the lid of the satchel shut tight, but it was too late. A huge, dark shape of impossible fuzziness slipped out of it like a live shadow and landed on four feet on the ground in front of her, tail straight and puffed out like a bristle brush. Scrat glared around and hissed. People gasped – some even cried out. They dragged their children closer, drew back. Birgit looked terrified. She let out a scream.

"It's OK, it's only Scrat," said Erskin into the crowd, though her voice came out as a tiny mouse-squeak. "He's a cat. He's probably just scared..." Erskin could see the fear on the faces of the villagers, could see them staring at Scrat's teeth, which were slightly longer than they should be. He didn't look anything like the scrawny village cats. And he had patches of silver that seemed to change depending on the light; today he had one on his chest that looked almost exactly like a crescent moon – a sign of bad luck in Lofotby. Bringing him here was turning out to be a serious mistake. She looked Scrat in the eye and said his name as firmly as she could manage. "Scrattletak." But Scrat bent low to the ground and mewled again. It was a strange, strangled sound that filled Erskin with a surge of dread. What on Yor was wrong? Was it really just the crowd?

The villagers were all terrified and getting louder. They feared the mountain creatures, Erskin knew, and in the current climate even a daft cat like Scrattletak could be mistaken for one of them. And worse, making that strange noise… Even the ground underfoot seemed to hum with the villagers' fear – to vibrate. If she didn't act now, Erskin was scared they might chase Scrat away somewhere – or hurt him. She must get him home, right now.

Erskin knelt and reached towards the mewling, spitting furball before she had time to worry about getting clawed. At her touch, Scrat froze. *Relax, Scrat,* Erskin thought. *I know you're afraid, but I won't let you get hurt. Climb into the satchel.* As always, he seemed to understand her thoughts – or it was probably just that she was lifting the satchel's lid and smiling encouragingly. Either way he shot into it like a flash.

As soon as Erskin stood up, Birgit hooked her under the arm. She could hear people whispering again:

"Who keeps a cat in a satchel like that...?"

"It looked like she was talking to it."

"Seemed to understand her."

"Could be hex magic!"

The whispers grew louder until they filled Erskin's head to bursting. They seemed to cling onto the back of Erskin's jumper like sticky threads, unravelling from the villagers' mouths as she moved and tangling her up.

"Come on. *Now*," Birgit's voice broke in, dragging Erskin back to reality.

Everyone had stared in silence as the sisters marched away, but then the whispers started to unfurl again. "Blummin' weirdo," someone close by muttered, loud enough for Erskin to hear. "Ought to be ashamed."

More cries were going up among the crowd now.

"Did you get a good look at that thing? Never seen anything like it..."

"It looked dangerous!"

Birgit doubled her pace, dragging Erskin along with her. She was relieved when they finally managed to leave the market square behind, and she could breathe the fresh, damp air of the fields. But the minute they were out of the glare of others, Erskin had a different problem. Birgit rounded on her.

"Erskin. WHAT is that thing? Where did it come from?" Birgit hissed.

Erskin's stomach lurched. It had all gone so wrong. How could she have been so stupid? Only her dad knew about Scrat. He had let her keep him in the barn when he saw how much it meant to her not to let the frail little kitten starve. He even helped her leave out food sometimes. But he'd made her promise never to pick Scrat up, because he was half-feral and should stay that way – *"Respect its nature, Erskin,"* he'd said. And he'd made her double promise not to show Scrat to anyone, because they simply wouldn't understand.

Well, he'd been right about that.

"If you want people to think you're weird, that's up to you, Erskin," Birgit went on. "But do you ever think for a second how it makes the rest of us look? Mother, and Father? *Me?* There's something actually wrong with you."

Erskin felt the pressure of everything she wanted to say, of the unfairness of it all, build up painfully in her throat. They, the children of the Mountain Keeper, would never be accepted by the village anyway, so why shouldn't she keep a pet?

Scrat wasn't dangerous. He was only a cat. He'd probably come off one of the few trade boats that made it into the harbour. But as outer-edge dwellers they lived too close to the mountain and so everyone thought they were infected by its hex magic. Erskin could be the most ordinary person alive and still never change their minds. She was destined to a life of being whispered about, and asked ridiculous, snarky things, like, "Aren't you afraid you'll get eaten by the cloud dragon?" Even though no one had seen it in years.

"Are you even listening to me?" Birgit asked, waves of dark hair trembling round her face. Birgit had hair just like their mother – the same as the Skollish people of the distant highlands, beyond the mountain, where their mother was born – before she'd made Lofotby her home. It was totally unlike Erskin's mousy mess and freckles. Birgit had the same ice-blue eyes and fine features as their mother, too – rather than the deeper, murky grey of Erskin's, which were much more like her father's. But other than looks, Birgit and their mother were not alike. Their mother was kind, and warm, with an adventurous spirit, and Birgit was—

"Well?" she screeched. "Stop ignoring me! Where did it come from?"

"He's not an 'it'," said Erskin, simply. "He's called Scrat."

Birgit flushed pink and went on. "I don't care what it's called. It's not normal, Erskin. People round here keep cats for one purpose only: killing mice. Not to make friends with... Maybe you really are hex-addled like they all say." Birgit looked down her nose at Erskin in disgust before she flicked her hair and marched off, back in the direction of home.

Even a punch to the stomach wouldn't have hurt Erskin as much as that did. *Hex-addled.* Tears welled in her eyes. The worst thing was, what if it was true? What if living under the mountain really had made Erskin this way, like everyone said – so strange and awkward and different? She glared at the hateful thing: the cause of all her problems.

Dayspring was close now, and mist shrouded the looming shape of Mountainfell in vast rings. She would run away from it if she could, but where would she go? It cut them off from everything beyond as if it *wanted* to trap them, and passage on board any of the trade ships came at a high price: money she didn't have. Besides, leaving would mean abandoning her family, and she could never do that. There was simply no escape.

Once Erskin had dried her tears on the sleeve of her jumper, she peeled back the lid of her satchel to peek inside. Two round, amber eyes stared back, like full harvest moons in an inky black sky. Scrat tilted his head and made a *Prrow* noise.

"Oh. You're acting all innocent now, I see," Erskin said, though she couldn't help a weak smile.

"Prrrow?"

Erskin smiled wider and gave Scrat a tickle between the ears. "You're trouble, Scrat," she said with a sniff. But Scrat's eyes closed, and he started to purr. She sighed. There's no way she could hold a grudge against Scrat. He was just like her: a calamity, but a well-meaning one.

Scrat's ear twitched and, in a flash, he'd opened his eyes to peer over the rim of Erskin's satchel, back the way they had come. When Erskin followed his gaze, she saw something slip behind a tree... A shadow of some kind. What, though, or who? Her skin prickled.

She watched the tree for a moment longer, holding her breath. But nothing else moved. Perhaps she'd just imagined it. Anyway, Scrat had a habit of this sort of thing – suddenly staring wild-eyed at nothing until she looked herself, then licking a paw in a smug way as if to say, *Tricked you*. He'd already settled back down again as if nothing had happened.

With great care, Erskin replaced the lid of her satchel and followed her sister – now a distant, faraway figure holding the glow lamp that was as bright as a star – across the fields. She was met by another light, just outside the cottage that was their home in the shadow of the great perimeter wall.

3

THE MOUNTAIN KEEPER – ERSKIN'S FATHER – looked grave when Erskin reached him across the mist-pooled fields. He held his lamp up, casting a light over them. And judging by the looks on their faces, Birgit had already told him her version of events.

Internally, Erskin simmered. Every time she looked at her sister, she remembered what Birgit had called her. *Hex-addled*. Erskin narrowed her eyes. She didn't want to see or even think about Birgit for the whole rest of the day.

"What's all this Birgit tells me about you bringing Scrat to the market, Erskin?" said her father as she got closer. "I agreed that you could keep him around as an *exception*, you know that."

Birgit gasped, horrified. "You *knew*?"

Their father squeezed the bridge of his nose. "I—

Yes, Birgit, I knew he was hanging around, but your sister promised me she wouldn't... Listen, I'll explain later." He straightened, and directed his stern frown at Erskin again. "It's one thing to let Scrat sleep in the *barn* and give him scraps to eat," he went on, "but a totally different matter to—"

He stopped after a glance at Erskin, on the brink of tears again, and at Birgit, so flustered and scornful. Instead of going on he sighed, planted his hands on his daughters' shoulders and rested them there, heavy, warm and soothing. He would often do this. Wrap them both up in his presence as if it were a blanket, drawing them in. Pulling them all together inside it. "All right. All right," he said. "Never mind. There's no harm done."

"No harm done?" cried Birgit, choking back emotion. "Dad, you should've *seen* it. And the way everyone reacted, it was so humiliating."

Erskin gritted her teeth.

"There's no point dwelling on that now," their father said softly. "It's done." Erskin buried her face in the softness of his dressing gown and breathed in its smell. Spruce trees and sweet vanilla. He must be exhausted from watching the mountain all night; poised to ring the warning bell at the first sign of danger. Since the tremor in the early hours, he'd been on the wall. He worked hard enough as it was, without all this to worry about too. He was barefoot, Erskin noticed when she glanced down. And, now she looked closer, she could see that he'd put his old grey dressing gown on inside out.

"So, what news from the Lordsson?" Their mother appeared in the doorway, fully dressed and surprisingly bright-eyed, considering the time.

"That it's probably just an earthquake," Erskin piped up.

"Nonsense," their mother scoffed. She'd never had much time for the Lordsson. She still talked about him as an entitled little boy in the year below her at school who, when she'd first arrived, had been *very* keen to let her know he'd one day be in charge. *He fancies his barra,* she'd say. "There's something stirring on that mountain," she added. "Something bad, and he knows it. Or he would do if he wasn't always sailing off to rub shoulders with the mainlanders, or whatever it is he gets up to. Come on, get inside for breakfast, you two. We'll all need to take turns on the wall today, to help your father." She drew her eyebrows together very slightly as her gaze flickered over him, but only Erskin seemed to notice.

"Mam, Erskin has a weird pet and she just let it loose at the market – in front of *everyone*," said

Birgit. Erskin gasped. The simmer inside her became a roil ready to boil over in seconds. How dare Birgit! Her sister hadn't managed to get her in trouble with Dad, so now she was trying it with Mam. Erskin was so angry she felt dizzy. She'd get her back for this...

A commotion of wriggling came from inside Erskin's satchel. Of course Scrat would choose now to want to be let out. She knelt quickly and opened the lid, but Scrat shot out like a swarm of bees, careering towards the wall and out of sight behind the house in a streak of black. Birgit screamed and their mother leaped back, while their father squeezed the bridge of his nose again and sighed. Erskin just stared after him. What had got into that cat today? Perhaps it had been the tremor. Sometimes farm animals reacted strangely to things like that.

"See," screeched Birgit. "I *told* you! It's probably diseased or—"

Once she'd recovered from the shock, her mother's hands went to her hips. "Erskin..."

Erskin opened her mouth to protest, and stopped. It was odd, but she was sure she could feel something happening under her feet. A strange rumble, like a vibration that was rising up through her legs. The realization that she'd felt this same thing in the market square hit her like a lightning bolt. It was when everything had gone wrong with Scrat – and now he was acting strange again. Is *that* what was upsetting him – the odd rumbles? At the time she'd thought it was something to do with all those people talking at once. But there were only four of them now, and it was definitely coming from the ground. It wasn't like last night's tremor, though: not a constant shake that grew in strength, but a subtle vibration that rose and fell. Like the echoing blows of a huge hammer. Or the slow, far-off footfall of a giant.

Her father frowned. "What is it, Erskin?"

She stared up at him. "Can you feel that ... shaking?" The whole family were silent for a long time as they tried to feel what Erskin could.

Eventually her father shook his head. "I can't feel anything."

"Oh, she's just putting it on," Birgit snapped. "It's *always* like this when she gets in trouble. She's just trying to distract..." Erskin ignored her. The grass around her father's bare feet was trembling very slightly, she was sure of it.

"Birgit, perhaps you'd better take your sister inside, in case it's the start of another tremor," said their mother, Scrat all but forgotten. "Your father and I—"

"Wait," said their father. "I think I can feel it

now too. It's not like the tremor last night, but there's definitely something happening..." They were all silent again, watching the ground. Erskin had felt a surge of it again as well.

"Girls. Inside," said their mother again. Without waiting for a response, she and their father ran up the stone steps that led to the top of the wall – and the lookout post – leaving Erskin and her sister alone.

Of course, Erskin went after them.

"What are you doing?" Birgit called from behind. "Stop! Mam said to go inside. Why do you *never* listen?" But Erskin had already switched off her ears. It was probably a good thing, because if she'd had to hear Birgit any more, she might've hit her.

Then Birgit screamed. Erskin couldn't ignore that.

Behind her, Birgit was trembling and pointing at Erskin's feet. She looked down, just as a huge spider scuttled across her shoe. Its legs were long, hairy, and striped with luminous blue, and it was enormous – the span of an adult's palm.

Erskin yelped and shook it off. Her heart hammered. She'd never seen a spider that size or colour – ever.

"Look!" shrieked Birgit. This time she was pointing at the wall. Erskin blinked, trying to make sense of what she was seeing. The bricks appeared to be moving. Then, finally, she understood.

The whole surface of it was crawling with the huge, blue-striped spiders.

4

Spiders were pushing through the gaps in the wall. A second ago there'd been none. Now there were hundreds – with more coming every moment.

Not just spiders, either. Creatures that looked like centipedes coiled out of the cracks, their little orange legs flailing as they pushed through and plopped onto the ground. Horrible big beetles scuttled towards her feet. Erskin's stomach lurched. The grass was crawling. *Everything* was crawling.

Not one single creature had ever made it across the wall before and now there were thousands. What did it mean? The wall had always been a precaution, built after their ancestors first crossed the mountain two hundred years ago – if we kept to our land, they would keep to theirs – and now...

"Mam!" Erskin cried. "Dad!" No answer came.

Couldn't they see what was happening from up there? Was it not happening on top of the wall? She had to tell them. They *had* to ring the warning bell…

Without daring to look where she was stepping, Erskin pelted as fast as she could through the writhing grass to the stone steps, which were – thank Life – mostly clear, and raced up them. She could only vaguely hear her sister now, calling out from behind.

"Erskin." Erskin's mother caught her by the shoulders the moment she reached the top. "Get back down those steps, right now. It isn't safe." She sounded breathless. "Something … strange is happening." So she *had* seen the spiders. "Go inside with Birgit and lock the door. Do you hear me?"

"Where's Dad?" Erskin spluttered.

"He's going to ring the bell. Now will you please—"

Erskin craned round to see her father dashing for the belltower. It looked like hard going. There were spiders up there, too, though not as many – and of course he had bare feet. Erskin gasped in horror, terrified he'd be bitten. Her mother's grip on her shoulders tightened as she watched him dodge through the spiders, but she didn't make a sound. Finally he made it.

The first peals of the bell rang out. It was louder than anything Erskin could have expected. She covered her ears, but the sound travelled through her whole body and shook her from the inside out. It seemed to go on for an eternity.

Then, silence.

After a long wait, Erskin uncovered her ears and opened her eyes. The spiders and all the other crawling creatures were gone, hidden away, as if they'd never been there. It was as if it had been a bad dream, an illusion – but it hadn't been. Had the noise from the bell frightened them off? Was it over now? Were they safe? Somehow their abrupt disappearance was just as eerie as their sudden arrival had been. Knowing they could hide so easily made Erskin shiver to her core.

Erskin was trying to make sense of it all when her skull began to ache. She drew in her breath and clutched her head.

"Are you all right? Speak to me." It was her mother's voice again, close to Erskin's ear. She tried to answer, but her thoughts had dimmed, as if pulled out of reach by some force, and into shadow. It was worse than the bell: like nothing she'd experienced before.

"I..."

From the other side of the wall came a sound that chilled her. A long, low howl.

Then the mountain slopes came alive. Trees rustled. Strange, indistinguishable shapes emerged from the mists and the undergrowth that seemed to watch them. Far larger and even more frightening than the spiders and insects, and they seemed to be staring at her. Eyes gleamed in the shadows beyond the wall. Everywhere Erskin looked, something looked back. Her head spun with terror and pain.

"I'll take her," Birgit said to their mother, and grabbed Erskin's arm. Erskin hadn't even noticed her arrive, but now the glare of Birgit's glow lamp dazzled her. Birgit sounded hoarse and breathless – whether with fright or from running up the steps, Erskin couldn't say. Perhaps she really should go inside now. She tried to move, but greyness seeped into the edges of her vision.

"What's going on?" asked her mother through the blur. "Erskin?" Erskin put a hand up to her temple. In the place of her thoughts was an urgent babble, like hundreds of voices, far too loud and garbled to make out.

She felt her mother touch her arm, but couldn't unclench her jaw to speak. All Erskin could do was groan as the babble in her head formed into something that her mind felt on the cusp of translating – but couldn't.

"Wait. What's that?" she heard Birgit say through the noise. "That … shaking?" And then Erskin felt it too. Vibrations coming up through their feet, just like earlier – only this time much, much stronger.

It was hard to pinpoint exactly what made Erskin look up at that moment. But she did.

Far, far above, on a mountain ridge as high as Erskin could see through the mist and shadow-light of dayspring, one great, white, scaled limb with gleaming, near-translucent claws appeared. It was followed by a second. Next to rise was the beast's head: wide, with big, dark eyes, a pointed snout ridged with spikes, and flared, gecko-like nostrils. Except this creature was huge. Even from such a vast distance it seemed to loom over everything.

Erskin's legs quaked. This had *never* happened before. Only in stories. Terrifying stories.

It was the cloud dragon. It couldn't possibly be anything else.

5

THE DRAGON ROARED. THEN IT PUSHED OFF AGAINST the ridge and rose into the air. As it did so, Erskin could swear the stone under her feet moved again. So it was the dragon moving that had been causing the vibrations – and Scrat's strange behaviour was because of it. Around her there were shouts and screams – some human, and the rest from other creatures. But she was too busy staring to concern herself with that now. The cloud dragon's thick, snake-like body just kept coming and coming, coiling up into the air where it hovered menacingly. Erskin felt frozen with fear. She couldn't even make herself breathe. Vaguely, she became aware that her mother was praying. As long as Erskin had known her, her mother had never done such a thing. Panic welled up in Erskin's throat.

Another roar came from the sky above them, where the cloud dragon now circled. As if responding, the whole mountainside echoed with the inhuman sounds of the other creatures. Was the strange thing happening to Erskin's head affecting them, too? Finally Erskin's father must have recovered from the shock, because the warning bell rang out again. It sounded louder than ever. The enormous dragon turned sharply in the air. Erskin's stomach flipped as its giant face tilted towards them. *Oh, no.* Had the bell caught its attention?

Its eyes searched around intently – until it found Erskin, Birgit and their mother.

The cloud dragon had seen them. The fearsome, flesh-eating Wyrm of the Mountain. At that size it could swoop on them in a matter of moments. It surged forwards. Erskin couldn't move. It was going to eat her, she knew it.

"Go!" Their mother shoved the children towards the steps. That snapped Erskin out of it – just in time to see her mother sprint across the wall, flailing her arms and shouting. Erskin's father abandoned the bell and stumbled out onto the wall, waving and yelling too. *No.* Her parents were trying to draw the dragon's attention in order to save her and Birgit.

"Dad! Mam!" But the cloud dragon had already

turned its gaze away from the sisters. Now it was fixed on their father. It seemed impossible that something so huge could focus on anything as small as one person, but it had. Erskin's stomach turned to lead.

The great beast sliced through the air at alarming speed until its shadow fell over them all. Everything happened at once as Erskin watched, unable to make it stop. The cloud dragon descended on the figure of her father, its eyes gleamed and Erskin cried out, sure she was about to see her father get eaten alive in one gulp.

Her father staggered backwards, tripped – and fell from the wall. They heard him land with a thud. Erskin felt winded. Birgit and their mother screamed.

There was no time to process what had just happened, however. In a split second the cloud dragon changed course – heading towards their mother. She threw herself down onto the flat stone of the wall, and the dragon changed course once more. It rose straight into the sky and rolled back on itself, the rest of its long body uncoiling metres away. A sigh of relief shuddered out of Erskin's body. The cloud dragon had spared her mother. It looked as if it was retreating.

Erskin made to run for her mam, but Birgit grabbed her arm, yanking her back. "Do as you're told for once and get in the house," she growled, shoving the dazzling glow lamp in her face so that her eyes hurt. "Don't be a hex-addled fool." All of Erskin's terror turned instantly to white-hot rage.

She wrenched out of Birgit's grasp, all else forgotten, and shoved her, hard. "Don't call me that!" Birgit turned pale and tried to stammer something, but Erskin was too angry to listen.

"You aren't Mam, so don't tell me what to do. I wish you didn't exist!" She shoved Birgit again, even harder, so that she fell over, the glow lamp held aloft. A breeze whistled past Erskin's ear. She turned to see luminous scales, inches away from her face. Attached to the dragon's serpentine coil of body came its infamous claws.

Out of sheer reflex, Erskin ducked – just in time. Birgit, on the other hand, couldn't get to her feet fast enough.

The dragon snatched Birgit up and carried her away. Erskin tried to scream but no sound came out. In a few seconds the cloud dragon was a pale streak across the sky, barely distinguishable from the mist except for the shining of the glow lamp that Birgit still held, even now. A few seconds more and it had disappeared behind the ridge entirely – carrying her sister with it.

6

For a moment Erskin couldn't believe what she'd seen. It *couldn't* be true. Her sister ... gone.

A ghastly hush fell over the mountainside. The menacing forms that had howled and snapped and snarled from the slopes slid into shadows – into undergrowth – and disappeared, as if following the dragon's lead. Erskin's head no longer pounded with noise put there by something that wasn't her. The eerie silence settled over everything while she absorbed the horror of what had just happened.

Tears stung Erskin's eyes and burned in her throat. It was all her fault. If only she'd gone inside when Birgit told her, it would never have happened. The way she'd shoved Birgit – and those terrible things she'd said to her before she was taken... What had Erskin done?

Something moved at the corner of Erskin's eye: her mother was running towards her. Erskin held out her arms for the fierce hug she felt sure was coming, but her mother pushed straight past without a word and ran down the steps. Erskin felt numb and unreal – as if she might float away in the breeze. It hit her with sudden, startling clarity, that her mam blamed her for what had happened too. She'd never been more certain of anything.

It came back to her then: her father. The fall. Peering over the ledge, she could see him sprawled on the ground outside their cottage, the door still open, swinging slightly in the breeze like an open mouth. She watched her mother fall to her knees beside him. "Lorens." Her mother's voice shook as she stroked his hair. "Can you hear me? Lorens?"

When Erskin's father finally groaned, a rush of relief swept through her. Thank Life, he was alive! But the relief quickly faded. He'd fallen before Birgit was taken. That meant he didn't know. When her father came round properly and found out what Erskin had done, wouldn't he hate her too? Her mother hadn't even looked at her this whole time and the shame of it all was overwhelming. Erskin wished she could take back the words she'd spat at Birgit; the push that had knocked her down so she couldn't get back up in time.

"Mam, I'm sorry," Erskin stuttered. "About Birgit. I'm sorry, it was my fault, I—"

"I can't think about that now," her mother snapped, her voice trembling. "I just can't…" She shook her head as if shaking away the thoughts, and then said more softly, "Help me with your father, Erskin. Go inside and fetch…" Her mother's voice drifted in and out of Erskin's awareness, but nothing felt real and she couldn't believe her mother was really talking to her. She'd pushed past her. She couldn't look her in the eye. There's no way she would ever be able to forgive her, unless…

Instinctively, Erskin stepped back. Far across the shadowy fields, help was starting to flock towards the wall. They must have heard the bell, seen what the dragon had done, and were finally coming – but for what? More standing around and arguing about what to do, after they'd helped her father, consoled her mother? None of that would solve anything. Surely they'd witnessed Birgit being carried away just as clearly as she had.

Erskin shook her head. No. She wouldn't accept that Birgit was gone.

There was no time to waste. It didn't matter that Erskin was so numb from the shock that she couldn't feel her legs properly. She *had* to save her sister.

A small voice said Birgit was already dead, eaten by the dragon or crushed in its claws, but Erskin pushed it deep down inside. With her mother and father occupied and the villagers still far off, she could slip away, go after her sister – but she would have to do it now.

With a floating feeling, Erskin ran to the rope ladder they kept fixed on top for emergencies and for maintenance work, and unrolled it on the mountain side of the wall. Its wooden slats clattered against the stone. Without hesitating, she started down the rungs.

"Erskin. Wait!" It was her mother calling her, but hearing her name just made Erskin's heart sting with shame. It made her want to get away faster.

"Stop," her mother was calling now. "Stop!" But she didn't follow Erskin, and her voice grew muffled behind the wall, which was better. Erskin didn't stop. If she left right now, there might be a chance to save Birgit. Erskin could still put this right.

At the bottom of the ladder, she took her first ever paces on the mountain side of the wall. The coarse grass crunched with frost and icy cool air curled around her ankles, like fingers taking hold. She could still just about make out her mother's voice behind her, crying out her name as she ran.

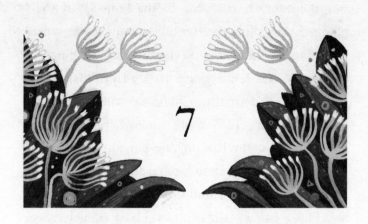

7

A LONG DEEP DITCH THAT RAN THE LENGTH OF THE
wall blocked Erskin's path. She had to get over it fast,
in case anyone decided to try to stop her.

Erskin eased herself down the steep, rocky slope.
Her legs trembled as she stretched in search of secure
footing on the slippery rocks, and her stomach turned
every time she sent stones skittering down into the
ditch. The bottom of it seemed a long way. Time had
filled in many gaps with silt, however, and smoothed
off the sharpness with moss, so it wasn't the challenge
it would've been when the early settlers of Lofotby first
dug it, in spite of Aleksander's regular maintenance.

It was cold at the lowest point, where shadows
lingered – she could feel the iciness radiating from
the frost-covered stones around her that barely ever
saw light. Gripping them to clamber up the other

side made her hands ache to the bone, as if she'd plunged them into the freezing stream water where the villagers gathered to do their weekly washing.

Worse, she felt a sharp pain in one hand that instantly began to throb, sending waves of agony down her arm, each more intense than the last. She glanced at the back of her hand in time to see a horrible insect flying away, and an angry welt rising on her skin where it had been. She couldn't believe it. She'd been stung – already. In her ears came strange, gloating whispers – that of a woman – though Erskin couldn't make out the words, and she was sure it had to be some strange effect from the pain.

But there was no stopping now. She just had to grit her teeth and keep on climbing.

Once on the other side, Erskin set off at a run. The dragon's nest was said to be at the very top of the mountain, and that surely had to be where it was taking Birgit, so that's where she would go. She couldn't bring herself to glance back at the wall for a final time. To see it from the wrong side. There's no way she could face her parents – or anyone from the village – ever again. Not without Birgit. So Birgit had better be alive, she thought. She felt the enormity of what she was doing like a cold pebble sitting in the pit of her stomach, though she couldn't afford to think about it too hard. Instead, she plunged on through tears and brambles, until she found a small, naturally curling path that took her up steeply.

The village receded from view quickly, and the wilderness crowded in with a kind of waiting silence. She was certain it was getting darker, in the thicket. The base of her neck prickled as though the skin there could sense she was being watched – followed – but she didn't dare look around for fear of what she might see. If something was going to leap out and eat her, she'd rather it just did it without her knowing too much about it beforehand. She wondered if any of the "offerings" to the dragon had found themselves on this path, too, and how far they'd actually managed to get. Maybe that's why the dragon had come to the village – because its meals hadn't been reaching it...

Slowly, as if the mountain were testing its voice, the silence broke. Erskin's head was a jumble and her heart pounded at the slightest noise, expecting the huge, looming bulk of the cloud dragon to reappear at any moment. She was certain she could hear it calling out occasionally, although it was hard to make out when the sounds of the mountain were all so strange and unfamiliar.

That wasn't the worst of it either. The little path she was on threaded round in such odd ways that it was hard to tell how close anything was – or how far. She was *sure* she could hear something behind her every now and then – a rustle, a cracking twig – but she told herself it was nothing. Still, with sick dread, she remembered the things that had emerged from the shadows, from the bushes, when the cloud dragon called. A noise came from the undergrowth up ahead. Erskin stopped dead, her heart pounding. As she watched with horror a small, black shape squeezed through a hatch of twigs – a black shape like liquid shadow – before it plopped itself inelegantly onto the path in front of her. Two amber eyes as round as coins looked up at her from within a ball of fuzz.

"Prrow."

Erskin gaped. "Scrattletak."

"Prroo-oow!" He sounded annoyed as he ran to Erskin and raced up her leg, claws digging in. It was no wonder all her clothes were full of holes and pulled threads. In this light it looked like he had silver markings on his front feet, as if wearing little walking boots – the crescent moon from earlier nothing but a mere smudge. In a flash he'd settled in place around her shoulders, whipping his tail round her neck like a big, hairy scarf. This is where he always sat when no one was around to see.

Sorry, Scrat, she thought as she reached up and

tickled between his ears. *I didn't mean to leave you behind.*

Scrat blew air out through his nose in a loud *huff* that sounded so grumpy it actually made Erskin forget everything for a moment and chuckle. Not for long, though – and it was with a stabbing pain that she remembered why she was there.

Scrat nuzzled her face with his warm, dry nose and it soothed her. They understood one another, Erskin could swear it. Birgit just didn't get it, because she didn't know him like Erskin did.

Guilt twanged inside Erskin for thinking badly of her sister after what had happened. Besides, she mustn't get distracted. She *had* to stay alert out here if she was going to survive for long enough to rescue her. *Please be OK, Birgit.*

It struck her that, although she knew her best bet was to reach the dragon's nest at the summit, she hadn't really considered how she'd get there. Going in the direction of "up" had been her only real plan... But she knew what Birgit would make of that: *Unrealistic. Clueless.* Still, it couldn't be much more complicated than that, could it? If she kept going up, sooner or later she'd surely reach the top. And, if she spotted the dragon in the meantime, she'd do her best to follow it.

She scrambled along a narrow pathway thick with scrub that seemed to wind back and forth in a zigzag. Erskin *thought* the path was leading up and, ultimately, would take her over the first major ridge. But she had to admit, it wasn't as simple or as obvious as that. The path weaved up, down and all over. Her cheeks burned with the shame of her growing uncertainty. Was she lost already? Her living scarf – Scrat – whisked his tail. At an exposed curl in the path, she could see the Mountain Keeper's cottage below. It startled Erskin to see her own home from above – so much smaller already. The village lay spread out beside it in miniature. Erskin imagined that she could pluck the school bell out of its tower and it would be the size of a pip in her fingers. The lights of the street lamps, the houses, the boats in the harbour, twinkled like a constellation. Beautiful. But eerie.

The first rays of sunlight broke through the sky's thick cloud and streamed across the mountain, oddly murky-golden up here, like marsh-light, but the village remained in stillness and shadow below, as if frozen in time. What was happening down there? she wondered. The market square was empty now. Were they all braced for another attack?

The wind picked up. Leaves of the nearby trees rustled. Erskin reached for Scrat. "Did you hear that?" They waited, as still as listening hares. But it must have simply been a breeze. Soon Scrat yawned and rested his chin back down on his paws.

Erskin hated her jumpiness, and wished she could get over the feeling that she was being watched. But the truth was those creatures she'd seen on the mountainside when the dragon came, the ones she'd heard howling and snarling after the tremor and had heard before on odd nights when she'd struggled to sleep, they were all here with her. Erskin wondered again what awful things those blue-legged spiders, twisting centipedes and nasty beetles from the wall could do. Did they burrow under your skin, or crawl into your ears while you slept? Perhaps they poisoned their victims. They would definitely bite. Bugs always bite. And bugs were now the least of her worries.

That line of daydreaming was getting way too terrifying, so Erskin changed her brain's direction. Why had the creatures come through the wall and appeared on the mountainside in the first place? What had brought the dragon down into the village? Was it related to the tremor?

There was no doubt that the dragon had been seeking out humans – and that the sound of the bell had drawn its attention. But why? Were the sacrifices no longer enough?

The breeze blew again through the trees, quickening Erskin's pulse. This time she was sure she could hear a voice carried on the air, too – a whisper, just like she'd heard when that thing had stung her hand – repeating words she could sometimes make out.

Leave here.

Go back, or...

... last chance!

At the same time the sting throbbed. A spell? There was talk of witches living on Mountainfell, as well as creatures. Aleksander the Lordsson's own sweetheart had fled here when it was discovered that she was a witch. Erskin stroked Scrat's tail, trying to soothe away her worries. There was no voice, she told herself. Only the wind. Things were bad enough without Erskin scaring herself as well.

But, voice or no voice, the painful cramping of her stomach brought her mind back to the fact that she had a long way to go, and not a scrap to eat.

8

SOON THE PATH PETERED OUT AND BECAME A STEEP
bank of rock and shale. Pay attention, Erskin! Don't
slip here! Erskin thought to herself, in Birgit's voice,
complete with her tone of disapproval.

Birgit. Her sister must be terrified, up in that
dragon's lair. Would it have eaten her yet – or was it
tormenting her, the way the farm cats did when they
caught a mouse? Erskin felt sick at the thought.

Away on the left was a cluster of trees. On the right
was a bush loaded with fresh dilberries. Seeing the
berries made her empty stomach cramp with hunger.
It had to be long past breakfast time by now and she
hadn't eaten a thing. Pushing away thoughts of her
sister for a moment, Erskin ran over to the leafy bush
and started plucking the dusky midnight berries, so
happy to finally have something to eat – but froze.

She stared at the berries. Her mouth was filling up with saliva, but what if these weren't dilberries at all, but something deadly? These definitely looked like dilberries, though. They grew all over the fields around the village and were as familiar to her as eggs from chickens. Surely she'd be all right with just a few? There's no way she could go on much longer without eating. She took a tiny bite of one. Flavour flooded her tastebuds: she'd never tasted such a delicious dilberry. Before she could stop herself, she stuffed the others straight into her mouth and collected more. They burst like juice bombs when she crunched them, the sweet, zingy taste tingling her tongue. Then she wrapped the rest in a tissue for later and turned to continue her journey.

Two eyes glared back at her from the bank. The creature slunk forward, its pointed snout wrinkled in a snarl. Its mottled coat was a muddy orange, mingled with dirty white and grey, and was mangy and matted in places. And its legs were bone thin and looked far too long for its body, so that it seemed to rise taller and taller the closer it came – the blackened claws piercing the dirt with each stride. It was wiry and tough-looking. It bared its teeth and growled. At the same time the sharp voice of the woman swam in the air around them.

Find the humans.

Drive them out.

Don't belong here!

All the hairs on Erskin's arms stood on end. What should she do? Stay frozen to the spot like this? Run?

The creature's eyes glinted with a kind of murderous light.

"Please," she said. "Don't kill me." The animal flattened its ears and snarled again. It swished its bushy, crooked tail. It looked almost like the foxes she'd seen in a book of fairy tales from the mainland – though she hadn't known for sure if such things truly existed. They were supposed to be cunning, but also shy, and in her book they avoided people – not like this one. Then again the ones in the story hadn't been this big or strange-looking, either. And then there was the voice, which had seemed to be speaking to *it*, not her... Terror rose in her throat so that the once-sweet taste of the dilberries burned. Her legs started to shake.

At her neck, Scrattletak stiffened, digging his claws deep into Erskin's collarbone. "Ouch. Be still, Scrat," she whispered through gritted teeth. Scrat hissed and Erskin swallowed her own terror, reached up and soothed between his ears. *Relax, Scrat. I know you're afraid. But I won't let it hurt us.* This worked a charm. Scrat settled down again, retracting those rose-thorn claws – though Erskin felt by the poise in his muscles that he was still half on his guard.

The fox-like beast sniffed the air. Is it hungry? Erskin wondered.

The animal took another step closer, never once taking its eyes off her. Slowly, Erskin reached into her pocket to find the dilberries. Her heart thundered in her chest but she tried to keep her voice level. "Here," she said. "Do you want this? It's food."

The creature looked at her, and Erskin couldn't explain it, but it was almost as if she could feel the whisper of its thoughts at her outstretched fingertips. And the whispers were growing louder – though she wasn't yet able to understand. It felt like dipping her fingers into a pool to test its temperature.

The fox flattened its ears and bared its teeth more broadly. Wow – they were sharp. Of course it didn't eat dilberries... Not with teeth like that.

Tears rose in Erskin's eyes. What could she do? Any moment now it was going to attack her. "Please," she begged it. "I don't mean any harm. Please just let me go." The creature stopped snarling and lifted its huge, pointed ears slightly. It took another cautious step closer. This near, Erskin could take in its long, slender snout with a glistening black nose and fine, white whiskers. The wisps at the tips of its oversized ears and its beautiful wood-brown, watchful eyes. When the light caught it just so, its dappled fur sparkled silver and bronze beneath the grime.

In spite of herself, she found it amazing. She'd never seen anything like it before.

And yet, was it supposed to look like this? Its pelt was filthy and practically hanging off its body, while its long legs strained under it, thin and fragile as dry twigs. When it moved she was sure she could see the shadow of its ribcage beneath the skin.

She felt something again – a connection as its mind whispered at the very limits of her reach – but just as she'd sensed its thoughts and started to feel her way through them, they were snatched away. It was like a steel door slamming shut.

Enough.

Trespassed.

No mercy!

That was the woman's harsh hiss and not the mind of the fox, Erskin was sure of it. The murderous glint came back to the creature's eye and it growled. Saliva dribbled from its mouth.

Out of the corner of her eye, Erskin saw one of the gangly, blue-striped spiders from before run right by her. As she watched, another emerged from hiding.

Now that she looked closely, the whole place was suddenly crawling with insects. She was sure they hadn't been there a moment ago. A shiver ran up her spine. It was just like before – down at the wall.

And there was something else too. The earth under their feet had started rumbling – *rumble, rumble, rumble,* like giant footsteps – just as it had down in her village outside her home. Erskin froze. A sharp pain sliced at her temple.

Bone-shaking roars followed from the skies, and a shadow fell over them.

It could only mean one thing: the dragon was on the move again.

Erskin strained to see it through the trees. If she could just see whether it still had Birgit in its claws, and whether she was OK...

Fear made Erskin feel light – brittle. The pain in her head stabbed again. The fox-like creature in front of her staggered and shook its head, as if the pain was affecting it, too. Then it fixed its eyes on Erskin and lunged at her.

Erskin sprang backwards. Its jaws clacked next to her arm, just missing her. She felt the whoosh of air from it. It lunged again and might even have caught her if Scrat hadn't leaped from her shoulders to stand in front of her, hissing and spitting.

"Scrat, careful!" But Scrat wasn't listening.

Everything happened as if in slow motion then. The creature's teeth snapped for Scrat's throat. Erskin surged forwards, shouting, *"STOP!"* She felt the word resonate in her mind, too; felt it cross the space between her and the creature. Something seemed to break. It was as if the steel door between them had melted away.

At Erskin's cry, the beast flinched in fright and twisted back on itself. She didn't wait to see what it did next. She scooped up Scrat and ran. She darted deeper under the cover of trees, dodging the dreaded spiders and insects wherever she could. Behind her, she heard a bloodcurdling yowl that was answered by a second. Something else yapped to the side of her, as if laughing.

At the very limit of her vision, she saw one of the fox-like creatures appear around a tree as if it had just materialized there, only to melt away again to nothing into the shade. Erskin gasped. How could it be possible? Just as she wondered if her eyes were playing tricks, another appeared out of nowhere, snapping beside her elbow. Its teeth clacked together three times, hard. Erskin screamed and gripped Scrat. She put on a burst of speed. The creature howled but clearly decided she wasn't worth the effort as its sprint became a trot. Then it faded away into the dappled shadows and vanished right in front of her eyes. There was no mistaking that it had simply disappeared. Not knowing where the animals were, or where they would appear next, flooded Erskin's senses with foggy terror. She surged forward. Scrat dug his claws in deep to cling on. She was tired. She couldn't keep running like this; her chest felt like it would burst. She needed a place to hide and rest. Erskin spotted a hollow tree up ahead and made a dash for it. It was just big enough for her to squeeze into, and she scratched herself against the rough wood in her haste.

Her head pounded and her ears thrummed with blood. It was damp inside the hollow, and cold. Thoughts rampaged through her mind. What if they found her in here? Then she would be trapped... A centipede crawled out of the wood next to Erskin's ear. She jerked back as it spiralled in on itself. She buried her hands in Scrat's fur and held her breath, listening out for any sign of the creatures and shuddering while the dragon roared and roamed the skies above.

9

WHEN ERSKIN FINALLY STOPPED SHAKING, AND THERE was still no sign that the creatures had followed her, she crept cautiously out of her hiding place. The dragon's roaring had first grown distant and then stopped altogether, and the throbbing pain in her head had finally eased. It was a relief – until she remembered Birgit.

Had the dragon left Birgit in its nest when it came out to circle the mountain just now, and is that where it had now returned? The rumour was that that's where it always took its meals, and why its nest was littered with bones... She hadn't been able to see properly through the tree branches but she didn't think she had seen her sister in its claws. Did that mean it had dropped her? Or worse?

It was Scrat who finally pulled Erskin out of the sea of her troubled thoughts. He slinked down from her shoulders, and crossed to a patch where the trees thinned.

"MOWWWW," Scrat cried. *"MOWWWW!"*

At first Erskin thought the fox-like creatures must have come back, but then she realized that, for some reason, Scrat was just in a temper. He shouted at her a third time, tail quivering as though he'd been given an electric shock.

"All right, all right," said Erskin with a gasp. "What's crawled up your bottom?" He swished his tail like an angry duster and shouted at her again before running further into the clearing. Actually, it looked like a path, of sorts, and it seemed to be going upwards. Had Scrat somehow found a route that led to the top of the mountain?

"Hold on, wait for me," said Erskin. "And keep your voice down." She didn't want those creatures to find them again, or to attract the attention of any others. She risked a final glance at the trees and their dappled shade, before following her impatient cat.

Scrat kept several paces ahead of her at all times. It was almost as if he knew where they were going – but that was impossible. Scrat had never been on the mountain ... or at least she didn't think so. The day he showed up at the cottage, tiny and half-feral, a lot of new ships had arrived in port. She'd just assumed he was a sea cat who wanted to try life on land for a bit. It was barely conceivable that he'd come from the *mountain*... But now, Erskin realized, she couldn't be certain. And she had to admit that she'd always known there was something that set him apart from the village cats. At the very least, he seemed sure of himself up here.

As they went on, the earth grew drier and drier. Worse, it became clear that the rock here was unstable. It gave under Erskin's feet, cracking and crumbling like chalk. Everything was so barren – from the pale trees jutting up like bits of twisted bone, to the grey dust that hissed like an animal and got in her eyes every time the wind blew. It would take just one wrong step for her to blunder into a ditch or twist her ankle in a crack.

As if that wasn't bad enough, the sting on her hand had started to throb with pain. She squeezed the small, angry-looking mound of flesh, eyes stinging with the agony of it. A little drop of something came out, that Erskin thought she saw sparkle gold. That was weird. She was sure the sting was the reason she kept catching snatches of the scary whisper, that she couldn't tell if she was hearing or imagining. But what of her experience when she'd faced the creature, Erskin wondered. That was even stranger. It had felt

as though she'd come close to sensing its thoughts...
But Erskin didn't even want to think about what that
might mean. *Hex-addled*, came her sister's words, as
if to taunt her, and inside she shrank a little more
with the shame.

Meanwhile, Scrat was moving further and further
ahead. Every time Erskin got close to him he darted
off. It was starting to get annoying. She wanted his
comforting warmth around her shoulders, like usual,
or to have him nestled snug in her satchel – not to be
following him around. Scrat was a cat, after all – he
might just as likely be chasing bees than leading her
anywhere useful.

Finally, Scrat stopped, plonked his bottom on
the ground and started to lick a paw. He was next
to something. Erskin shielded her eyes to see. It was
hard to make out at first, being half-hidden by the
remnants of a tree, but it was some sort of tall shape.

Erskin held her breath. Could it be another
creature? She couldn't sense any danger coming from
this thing, though. She recoiled at that, realizing that
she'd unconsciously stretched out to it with her mind.
What was going on with her? This had never happened
before she'd come to this awful place. Except with
Scrat, of course – but that was just because they were
in tune with one another, that's all.

She squinted, looked harder at the shape, moved closer. Actually, it looked like rocks, carefully stacked to create a conical shape. But what could have made it? Nothing formed like that naturally.

The stones were covered in crispy half-dead moss and one of them even had a weather-worn shape on it that looked carved – though she could only make out part of a swirl. "It's a cairn," Erskin said out loud, frowning, "and it's old too." Her Skollish mother had sometimes talked about cairns in the far-off highlands where she was born, before she'd come to Lofotby on her father's trade ship, met Erskin's dad, and settled there. Climbers left the cairns to mark safe routes for others. But that was impossible. No one came up here. The handful who did – those offered to the dragon in order to keep it away from the village – were never seen again. And if it had been those scientists from the mainland, there was no sign of them now.

Erskin didn't like the cairn, and she didn't trust it either. It gave her a bad feeling. "Come here, you," she said, picking up Scrat. "We were lucky this time, but I'm not risking getting lost by following you around." At first he dug his claws into the ground to resist, his body stretching impossibly long the more Erskin tried to lift him. Until finally Scrat gave up, and let himself be bundled into Erskin's satchel.

A path stretched on past the cairn to the other side of the ridge. From there, she'd be able to see the summit, and know how far it was. A growing doubt nagged at the back of her mind. What was she doing? What was she expecting to find at the peak? She didn't even know for sure that the dragon's nest was up there. It was just village rumour, and even then who was to say the dragon would have taken Birgit there? It crossed her mind that any chance of finding her sister alive was a fantasy – a false hope. After all, reality wasn't Erskin's strong point, as Birgit never failed to remind her.

Erskin clenched her jaw. She'd come this far, hadn't she? There's no way she could give up on her sister now.

Isn't that right, Scrat? Scrat was still grumpy about being shoved in the satchel, Erskin could tell, but he yawned and nestled down for a nap.

Once over the ridge, everything changed. Erskin's heart sank to see there was still no clear view of the summit. She'd been stupid to think it would be a short, easy climb up Mountainfell. Instead, the way ahead opened out into a vast dip that may once have been covered with dense fir forests. But now the trees were little more than white, branchless stakes, the ground dry and cracked.

A twig snapped behind her and Erskin swivelled round, heart in her mouth. But there was nothing there – at least, nothing she could see. From the very start of her journey, this place had made her feel watched... In fact, she'd had the same strange feeling even before she set foot on the mountain, ever since the market, she realized with a start. Erskin shook herself. Now she was just getting carried away. It was far more likely that those strange creatures who'd faded in and out of shadow had picked up her scent again, and were stalking her. Which, as it turned out, was an even less comforting thought than the first one. She carried on with a quickened step.

Erskin shivered as she walked. A chill wind whistled around the stumps and sapless white trees, blowing up yet more dust, but her shiver was more to do with the memory of the dragon replaying uninvited in her head. She couldn't stop seeing that huge, serpentine face bearing down on them. The tiny figure of her sister, as she'd been carried away. And what Erskin had said to her just before. She had to find her. Even though her legs ached more with every step, she was determined to reach her. Before the worst happened. Before—

The ground gave under Erskin's foot and she lurched back as dry earth crumbled. Her heart thundered: she was standing right on the edge of a wide rupture – and it was too deep and too dark to see how far down it went. There were cracks running out from it too – some parts hidden beneath dust and sticks. Erskin gasped. Beyond, the ground was a labyrinth of chasms, and what was worse it rose up steeply in juts of rock that she would have to climb.

She'd have to tread carefully from now on. *Very* carefully, if she wasn't going to fall.

IO

ERSKIN DID NOT WANT TO FALL. ALL SHE WANTED was to reach her sister in time. But to make matters worse the clouds had rolled over and the ground was cast with deceptive shadows. Erskin bit her lip.

"MOWWW," said Scrat, poking his head out of the satchel.

"Oh, Scrat. Don't start all that again," Erskin sighed. She peered around, searching for an easier crossing close by, but there was only this. She couldn't retrace her steps back to the cairn now. That might take ages, and Birgit needed her.

"Moowww," Scrat moaned.

"It'll be *fine*. Stop worrying. Just stay in my satchel while I climb over. You'll be safe, I promise." Was it her imagination, or could Erskin understand Scrat even more than she used to? She reminded herself that she must cut down on talking to him. It was becoming a bad habit. What would Birgit say?

It's not like what goes on in your head makes much sense anyway, she thought to him with a gentle smile. In response Scrat huffed at her through his nose and preened his whiskers. Erskin chuckled, then shook herself. Without meaning to, she'd gone and done it again… She hadn't been able to help it.

She couldn't think about that now, however. Now, she had to focus.

Erskin paced along the edge of the gap until she found where it was thinnest – barely the width of a stride. There, she stepped across. That was easy. But she didn't want to get carried away; she couldn't afford to slip – so she had to take it calmly.

Take it calmly. Erskin could do that. She turned her attention to the next hurdle. It was another smallish crack, but this time the rocky ground on the other side was raised. It would get even steeper as she went on.

Careful but quick. Careful but quick. And *concentrate*. Definitely that, too.

Erskin wondered what Birgit would do if she could see her now. She would absolutely lose it, that's what. She knew exactly what Birgit would say as well. "Why do you have to be so reckless and foolish all the time? You never listen. Why can't you just be normal?"

In spite of herself, a fog of anger descended over Erskin. It filled her head from the bottom up like a cup. For as long as she could remember, Birgit had treated her like an irritation who only existed to make life difficult. Well, she could look after herself. And she would prove it right now. When Birgit learned what she'd accomplished in order to reach her, to save her, she'd *have* to give Erskin credit.

Inside her satchel, Scrat shifted.

"Stop that, Scrat," she muttered. Her thoughts about Birgit had left her feeling bitter, unsettled. When the wriggling subsided Erskin reached down and tied her satchel shut, taking care to make sure Scrat didn't notice. Erskin knew from past experience how much he hated to be shut in, but if he leaped out or climbed onto her shoulders it could be disastrous, and she didn't have the energy to worry about that too.

Erskin crouched and leaned across the next gap so she could place her hands firmly against the rock on the other side before stepping across. She was really getting the hang of this now.

The side of the satchel bulged as Scrat moved around again. There came some scratching sounds, followed by a pause. Then a long, angry mew. That's when Erskin knew Scrat had discovered she'd tied the satchel shut.

I'm sorry, Scrattletak, but it's for your own good and it won't be for long...

She was higher up now, and the gaps between the rocks were getting much wider and harder to cross. If she could figure out the best route, she'd be fine, she told herself, but deep down she wasn't so sure. Dark shapes flitted around in the air – every now and then Erskin caught the sound of a flutter overhead. With a lurch of fear, she realized what they were: some sort of horrible, leathery-winged bats that were coming up from the dark voids. Every time she heard them squeak or one came too close it made her flinch.

Their high-pitched sounds bothered Scrat, too. He wriggled even more wildly. A paw poked through a gap in the satchel's lid, claws drawn, and raked at the material. He *really* wanted to get out. Tough, Erskin thought. It's too dangerous right now.

Erskin wove along the tops of the sturdiest-looking rocks. She was almost across. Just one more chasm to navigate, the biggest gap yet, and then she'd be on firmer ground. Erskin's legs trembled if she looked down into the dark depths, so she tried not to. The gap was too wide for her to reach across to steady herself, so she'd just have to jump. She wiped her sweaty palms against her clothes and held her breath, ready to make the leap.

Scrat scratched at the inside of the satchel and hissed. One end of the strap tore a little. Panic welled in Erskin's chest. She had to go quickly before he broke free and hurt himself.

Erskin took the jump. She made it – just. For one heart-stopping moment, she teetered on the edge of the chasm. Stones dislodged around her feet and skittered down and down into the darkness. She didn't hear them hit the bottom. Erskin finally caught her balance.

The ground started to shake. Oh, no. Not the dragon… Not now. For a moment Erskin felt frozen to the spot. The shaking was getting worse and worse. That meant it wasn't the dragon's booming footsteps, but another of the violent tremors, just like last night's. Her heart leaped into her mouth, but the previous tremor had lasted less than a minute. Perhaps if she just stayed where she was, she could wait it out?

Straight away Erskin knew she'd made a terrible mistake. A cloud of screeching double-winged bats flooded out of the chasm like a swarm of flies. Erskin screamed and flapped her arms. Just as the tremor reached its most violent peak, her satchel tore open and Scrat streaked out, saw the bats and the chasm, and scrambled desperately to cling on to the satchel.

At the same time a squealing shadow whizzed close to Erskin's eyes: another bat. Erskin screamed again and stepped back. There was a loud crunching, crumbling noise and with a sick thud in the pit of her stomach, Erskin realized that the ground was giving way.

Erskin threw herself towards the rock in front of her but missed by a long shot. Instead she clawed the crumbling ground, managing to cling to a tree root as everything else tumbled down. She dangled over the darkness as a chain reaction spread along the entire crag. Scrat let loose an unearthly shriek as he clung on with all his might – and claws – to the outside of Erskin's satchel.

But the jolt of it all and the weight of Scrattletak tore the rest of the satchel's strap. It came off her shoulder and dropped away. The last thing Erskin saw was the horror in Scrat's round amber eyes as he fell with it – disappearing into darkness.

II

"Scrattletak! Scrat!" Erskin screamed into the depths of the chasm, against the terrible rumbling sound as it opened into a wide, jagged, gulping void that stretched as far as the eye could see. But no answer came. At least, not from Scrat. A strange noise seemed to echo out from deep inside the darkness, beneath the squeals of the bats. Faint, but definitely there: a garble of angry words.

It was the same voice she thought she'd heard before: the woman's.

It echoed from all sides until Erskin couldn't tell if it was real or just in her head. Nor could she make out the words, only the wrath behind them. A coldness radiated outwards from Erskin's core until every part of her felt like ice, except for her hands, which burned with the effort of clinging on. Her grip around the tree root started to slip. She couldn't hold on much longer. With tears in her eyes, she turned her face to the sunlight above her, speckled with the last of the fleeing bats. It was the last time she'd ever see it.

A young face poked over the edge of the chasm, peered down at her, and blinked.

"Hold on!" said a boy's voice.

Two arms shot down and gripped Erskin tight. She gasped. How could this be real? Surely she had to be imagining it? But the hands that now wrapped around her forearms felt real enough.

"You'll have to use your feet too," said the boy, grimacing. "I'm not strong enough to pull you out on my own."

Erskin snapped back to reality and clung hard to the boy's arms so they were locked together, the tree root abandoned. She scrambled against the side of the chasm until she found her footing and used her legs to help push herself up. With that and the boy's help, she was soon lying on solid ground again, exhausted and gasping.

"The shaking started and I heard a shout," said the boy as they both recovered. He was sitting next to Erskin as he caught his breath. Beads of sweat edged along his hairline. "And then," he went on, "just as

I arrived around that rock – I saw you drop in." He fell silent again, watching Erskin.

"You're lucky I was here," he added.

Erskin's stomach lurched, remembering how Scrat had fallen. Instinctively she reached down to touch the satchel that usually rested against her hip – her satchel that was no longer there. "Scrat." Erskin's eyes filled with tears. *Scrattletak, can you hear me?* she thought desperately. *Are you alive?* But she couldn't sense him any more. He was gone.

"Are you … all right?" the boy asked gently.

"Scrat … he fell in," she said. "He's down there." She nodded towards the chasm.

"Oh," said the boy, his shoulders sinking. "Sorry. That's… I'm sorry." He hesitated, rubbed his head. "Is that your cat? The one from the market?"

Erskin nodded. She recognized him now – it was Leif, from the village. The boy she'd caught staring at her in the market. What was he doing here?

"You know, cats are good survivors," he went on. "There's this old saying I've heard that they actually have nine lives. It would be nice if that was true, wouldn't it?"

Erskin sniffed. "Do you think it is?"

"We're on a magical mountain. I'd say anything can happen."

Erskin smiled weakly, feeling a little better.

"Why *are* you here?" Erskin wiped her face.

Leif shifted and his ears went pink. He mumbled something about getting lost.

"Lost?" Erskin narrowed her eyes at him in disbelief. "How?" Was that even possible? The boundary between the village and the mountain was obvious. There was miles of wall between them. No one could wander past it by accident – and in the opposite direction to the village, where all the people lived.

His pinkness spread. "I … thought you might need help. When I saw your sister get taken, I…"

"But how did you see that? Could you tell from the village?" All at once she remembered the dark shape lurking in the shadows on their way home from the market, and then again on the mountain. "Wait a minute," said Erskin. "Have you been … following me?"

A million expressions rolled over the boy's face. For a moment he settled on offended, and puffed himself up as if he was about to object. But then all the air left him, and he rubbed the back of his neck.

"Yes." He sighed. "I did. I followed you. It was kind of an accident."

"An accident?" said Erskin. "You followed me home and then onto a dangerous mountain by accident?"

Leif huffed and looked even more embarrassed. "Now you're making it sound silly."

At any other time, Erskin would have laughed. But right now she felt too hollowed out inside. She remembered the look in Scrat's eyes as he fell. School, and the normal village life that Leif reminded her of, seemed like for ever ago. Like a distant dream, from before she lost her sister, and now her best friend.

Leif seemed to notice that her thoughts had turned dark, because in a small voice he said, "Um. I'm sorry about what happened to your sister and your cat. I love cats."

Erskin sniffed. "You – love cats? Really?"

Leif nodded, and then frowned. "I don't like it when they catch birds, though. Or mice. I like birds, and I sort of like mice too, though not really as much. I especially like birds and I don't like it when they get killed."

Erskin was confused. She'd never heard anyone speak about animals like this before. "But ... catching pests is what cats are supposed to do, isn't it?"

Leif shrugged. "Doesn't seem right to me. But I guess they can't help it. Just their nature, I suppose."

But Erskin's heart sank further, as she thought about Scrat's daft, loving nature and how most of the time he wanted nothing more than to sit on his perch around her shoulders and be given fuss. She couldn't bring herself to reply, so she changed the subject. "Why *did* you follow me all the way up here?" She eyed him – his short, neat black hair, his green eyes and faint freckles – but he didn't meet her gaze.

Eventually he sighed and scratched his forehead. "Well I always thought we could be friends," Leif said. "You don't really seem to fit in around the village. And that's great!" he added in a hurry. "Because neither do I."

Erskin frowned, but Leif carried on. "You always avoid me though," he said, scuffing the ground with his shoe. "And *then* I saw that creature at the market – Scrat. I'd never seen anything like it before. I just wanted to see it again, that's all. Find out more about it, you know? But then, the dragon came and, like I said before, I saw what happened to your sister. So, one thing sort of led to another – accidentally. When you ran onto the mountain, I thought you might need help."

"How did you stay hidden for so long?" she demanded.

Leif just shrugged. "Trees," he said.

"You hid behind trees?"

Leif nodded.

"And those creatures, back there. The ones that chased me. How come *you* didn't get attacked?"

"Er." Leif rolled his eyes, but not in a sarcastic way, more a "thinking" way. "I ... climbed a tree."

"And how did you cross the chasm without me noticing you then? Hmm?" Erskin raised an eyebrow. "That can't have been trees." She was actually beginning to feel quite impressed at how well he'd managed.

"I didn't," Leif said simply. "Looked far too dangerous. So, I followed the markers instead. You know. The cairn thingies. With those faded old symbols carved on them. I came out on a hidden path on the other side of all that just as the tremor started – and that's when I heard you call out."

Erskin gasped. "You found another one of the cairns? How?"

"I—"

But Erskin interrupted him immediately. "Let me guess. You climbed a tree?"

Leif nodded. "If in doubt," he said, "climb a tree. That's what I think."

For a while Erskin studied Leif in silence, unaware of the smile forming at the corners of her mouth. He was so unusual. Didn't it bother him, to be that way? Leif had been watching his surroundings, but when he turned back to Erskin his face was serious.

"Listen. No one knows this," he said, "so don't tell. But sometimes I sneak onto the other side of the wall."

Erskin's eyes widened.

"Not far," he added quickly, "only to a place where there's a nice field and some big trees. It's right next to the wall on the other side, and that part's not even the mountain – it's just a *field*, split in half. How can one part of the field be safe, when the other part isn't? Just because a stupid *wall* cuts through it." Leif puffed out his cheeks. He seemed to have startled himself with his own rant.

Erskin was aghast. "Why would you do that?"

"Because it's quiet." Leif shrugged. "I like people a lot, but sometimes I need a break from them, you know? I need *thinking time*." He drew out the words as if talking about something sacred. "There's no one around in the field wanting me to play or do stuff with them, no one to give me chores... I like to lie down in the grass there, listen to the birds and the wind in the trees. Sometimes I think so hard I even have a nap," he added. Then he flushed and scuffed the ground again, causing a plume of dust to rise.

For a while Erskin lost herself in thought. She couldn't believe Leif had willingly crossed the wall. What would the other villagers say? That he was hex-addled, for sure. But she understood it too, in a way. She'd been scared of the mountain her whole life, but also, secretly, fascinated by it. And she definitely understood the need to get away from people sometimes. A lot of the time in fact.

"That's what I always loved about Scrat. He understood me. Not like people in the village. Any of them…" Erskin bit the inside of her cheek as she remembered. Leif was so easy to talk to that she couldn't help but give away more and more things about herself. "Birgit didn't think it was right when she found out about me having him. She said it wasn't normal to…" But she couldn't go on: sorrow choked her words away.

Leif looked down and rubbed his arms. "Sisters," he said, shaking his head. "My sister and I are best friends – we do everything together. Well, not everything, but a lot of things. But sometimes she doesn't get me either … you know. Like" – he dropped his voice – "I'm not sure she'd understand why I like hanging out on my own in a field."

Erskin's chest felt squeezed. She knew Leif was just trying to make her feel better by suggesting it wasn't just *her* sister who didn't get her – but it was actually working a little bit.

"Your sister's called Yasmin, isn't she," she said. Erskin knew Leif's sister vaguely from school – but she'd only ever seen her from a distance, chatting with her friends.

At first Leif looked surprised that Erskin had noticed something about him – albeit only his sister's name – and then he beamed. "Yas is great. Hardly anything fazes her." Leif's relationship with his sister sounded so perfect. Erskin and Birgit didn't always see eye to eye. In truth, they didn't often like each other much at all. But that didn't mean Erskin wouldn't do anything to get her back.

"But, we don't get on all the time, obviously," he added, seeing Erskin's face. "She gets stressed out with me for doing the littlest things sometimes – like, climbing a tree." Leif rolled his eyes. "Says it's dangerous and I'll break my neck."

Erskin smiled. "Yes. Mine does that too."

"You must be really worried about her," said Leif, scratching at the old stump with his fingernail. "I know I would be. For what it's worth, I hope you get her back. I really do."

"Me too." Erskin sniffed. "Thanks," she added with a smile.

Leif cleared his throat. "We should really get away from the edge," he said, changing the subject. "In case there's another, I-don't-know-what-you-call-it. Landfall? If that's what they are. I didn't really believe what the Lordsson was saying about the tremor being natural – did you? And what about the dragon?"

Erskin could suddenly see why Leif's "thinking time" was so important to him – he had a lot of questions. But perhaps he was right. Since the dragon took her sister away, she hadn't really thought about anything apart from getting her back. Which meant she hadn't actually stopped to wonder why it had chosen now to come down the mountain, either.

Erskin nodded, frowning. "Something must have happened to make it turn up at the village," she said, puzzling it out. "Why now, after so many years?"

"Exactly." Leif's eyes widened, and he shuddered. "I couldn't believe it when it appeared round the big ledge. No one has ever seen it so close up – at least not in *our* lifetime." He shook his head. "You think you're safe, that it'll just be a normal, boring day, and then *bam!* A dragon. I thought…"

They moved further up the path as they spoke, but Erskin couldn't help glancing back across the maze of cracks and drops to where Scrat had fallen. A wash of pain rolled over her, remembering. But Leif was right – this whole place was too unstable. Much of the ground had fallen away, and the nearest split had widened. She could see now that there was no way past the chasm back to the village. But in spite of how dangerous it was to stay, she couldn't bear the thought of leaving the place where she'd lost Scrat.

Another burst of angry words caught on the breeze, quiet at first – rising out of the darkness of the mountain's belly. And then the faintest hiss of the same voice on the air – in Erskin's ears – but this time the words were clearer, as if spoken right in her ear: *"You don't belong on this mountain."*

It made Erskin's blood turn to stone. Erskin glanced at Leif, but he didn't seem to have heard. Erskin wondered why. Why just her? It had all started when she got that sting – and as far as she could tell Leif didn't have one. Something didn't want her here – that much was clear.

But Erskin refused to give up on Birgit. She couldn't let what had happened to her – to Scrat – be in vain. She'd stay on the mountain for as long as it took to find her sister. Even so, the thought of what the dragon would do if it caught her filled her with dread. Surely it was only a matter of time before that happened?

Together, Erskin and Leif left the chasm in search of the cover of trees, as the shadow of clouds rolled over them, and the wind began to bite.

12

"SO," SAID LEIF, AFTER THEY'D WALKED A LITTLE way. "If we go this way we should be able to get round that massive chasm so we can get back to the village."

Erskin stopped in her tracks. "Past the chasm? Back down?" She shook her head. "That's not where *I'm* going. I'm going up."

"Up?" Leif stopped too. He stared at her in disbelief. "You mean you haven't changed your mind, even after you almost died? And you still want to go up, towards that dragon?" He shivered all over.

Erskin couldn't believe her ears. "Of course! I'm going to rescue Birgit, my sister. Remember?"

For a moment they stared at each other in stunned silence. Then they both spoke at the same time.

"The dragon must have taken her to the summit, where it nests, and unless I get to her in time..."

"You can't still want to go up there after all that – back at the village the grown-ups will organize a search party for her and…"

They stared at each other again – even more horrified than before. This was exactly why she liked to do things on her own. People were so hard to understand. "I can't abandon my sister," said Erskin finally, and folded her arms. "You go back if you want, but I have to go on."

She'd never asked for his company. True, she'd been surprised by how easy he was to be around. And if it hadn't been for him, she probably wouldn't be standing here now.

A gust of wind blew across the dry earth, whipping up dust and carrying with it the stench of something vile and rotten from the dark trees up ahead. Erskin couldn't help but shiver, and she was sure that Leif did too. She wished she could just leave the mountain, but she wasn't going home without Birgit.

"Listen," said Leif, after a long pause. "I'll stick with you, because I don't think either of us stands a chance on our own in this place. But I'm not going anywhere near that dragon. I'm not letting it mistake me for one of the Lordsson's 'offerings'." He shuddered. "That's my final word."

"Fine." Erskin shrugged. "I never asked you to." She resented what he'd said about her not having a chance on her own. Though maybe he had a point. Some company might at the very least make the journey easier.

"Good," said Leif, beaming. "Excellent." He didn't seem to notice her resentment. Erskin wondered what it was like to be so cheerful all the time and not have to worry about everything. But then he wasn't the Mountain Keeper's child. People didn't automatically assume he was hex-addled.

Afternoon brought thick, yellowish mist, and a sweep of sparkling frost down on every surface. As much as Erskin wanted to go on, exhaustion and hunger forced them to rest by an old, decaying stump.

"You don't have any food with you, do you?" she asked Leif hopefully.

Leif rummaged in his pockets. He pulled out stones, twigs, a couple of feathers, and half a small biscuit wrapped in paper. They shared the morsel of biscuit, but it wasn't enough.

"Um. I do have these. I picked them earlier," said Erskin, taking the tissue pouch of berries from her pocket and unwrapping them. "But..."

"Dilberries!" said Leif. "Yum." He tucked into them before Erskin could mention that she'd picked them on the mountain. Not that it seemed like Leif would be bothered anyway.

From somewhere in the distance the cloud dragon roared. It was faint and far away, though Erskin hoped that didn't mean it was circling back on them – or the village, to carry away more victims.

"How are we going to find this ... lair, then?" asked Leif after he'd swallowed the berries and wiped his hands on his trousers. "Not that I'm going anywhere near it, you understand." His face had turned grave and he was watching the sky. It seemed to Erskin that the dragon was the only thing that visibly frightened him.

Erskin shrugged. "They say its nest is at the summit, so..."

"So...?"

"So, I'm heading towards the summit. You know. Up." Embarrassment burned in two hot circles on her cheeks now that the shakiness of her plan was fully revealed, but she did her best to hide it, and Leif didn't question her any further. "Anyway, it should be easy to find," Erskin went on, trying to convince herself as much as anything. "They say the closer you get the worse it smells, and that it's littered with bones. And … lots of other things." Erskin gave an involuntary shudder. It was true – the horrible stories about the dragon and its nest were almost endless. But perhaps it wasn't a good idea for either of them to think about those now.

Leif grimaced, and then shook himself. "I guess being the Mountain Keeper's daughter you know loads about the mountain, don't you? Way more than the rest of us. I didn't mean to be rude, so I'm sorry if I was. I'm sure you know where you're going."

Erskin flushed bright pink and looked away.

"What is it like for you, anyway," said Leif more quietly, "being the Mountain Keeper's daughter…?"

More heat rushed up the back of Erskin's neck. She should've expected this. It was never going to take long for the subject to crop up – and then he would use it to taunt her. Why had she ever trusted Leif?

"Horrible, what do you think?" Erskin snapped. "Everyone thinks I'm weird and…" She trailed off, fighting back tears.

"Well?" asked Leif gently. "Are you?"

"Am I what?"

"Weird…"

To her embarrassment, Erskin couldn't hold back any longer, and the tears ran down her cheeks. "Yes," she admitted, through sobs. "I probably am."

For a while, Leif didn't say anything at all. Erskin couldn't look at him – she was far too filled with shame. Then she felt his hand rest on her arm. "Sometimes," said Leif, "I like to talk to the trees in that field I told you about. Because they're the only ones who'll listen to all my questions without telling me to shut my trap and do something useful. Anyway, aren't most people weird, when they stop pretending?" He gave her arm a gentle squeeze, stood, and strolled on ahead.

Erskin wiped her eyes and nose on her sleeve.

Suddenly she felt more tired than ever, in an oddly relaxed way after her conversation with Leif. His presence was comforting. It would be so easy to close her eyes and drift into a still, grey, dreamless sleep. To just switch off and block everything out. But she couldn't. For Birgit, she had to keep going. And now, for Scrat too. It was her fault that it had all happened, and she couldn't let his loss have been in vain.

Without warning, the air felt too hot and thick to breathe, her clothes too tight. They seemed to constrict, like a snake coiling round her chest.

Trapped.

Erskin staggered to her feet and took deep gulps of the cold air.

"What is it?" asked Leif, turning back to glance at her. "What's wrong?"

Erskin didn't respond. She didn't know how to.

The patchy mist smelled, and even tasted, of wet soil and rotten things. They were in a dank, marshy place, where decaying remains were all that was left of many of the trees. Unlike the lower slopes that had been too dry for much to grow, up here beyond the chasms it was too marshy and wet. She rested her shoulder against one of the trees and tried to shake off the strange, tightening panic.

Leif came over to her, his forehead furrowed. "Are you sick?"

Erskin didn't answer. She closed her eyes, hoping it would block out the uncertainty making her tremble. But instead of calmness, something else came to her. Something terrible. A heartbeat, thumping hard and fast in the dark. And words.

Trapped... Get out!

Erskin jerked back and spun around, making Leif shriek – he'd come even closer while she'd had her eyes closed. But there was nothing, no one, there. Something was wrong – very wrong. A kind of raw panic she couldn't describe was rising up inside her.

"I..." How would Leif react if she told him she felt like she was trapped, like she couldn't breathe? Birgit's words swam into her head. *You wonder why everyone at school thinks you're weird... You're not normal.*

It was as if Birgit was right next to her, whispering in her ear. But Leif had said most people were weird. Still, doubt flooded her.

"I've got a headache," she said.

The voice, the feeling, intensified: *Trapped. Must get out.* Erskin's palms started sweating.

Leif narrowed his eyes, watching her. "You probably need water. Maybe there's some..." But Erskin had stopped listening.

That's when she knew what she had to do. She had to dig. There was no way to stop herself – it was as if she was no longer in control of her own actions. She dropped to her knees and started to burrow into the rich dark soil with her hands. Life knows what Leif was going to think. But she *had* to do it. She couldn't pretend that nothing was happening any more.

"No. Not here," she muttered under her breath.

Erskin looked around. Leif was staring at her, wide-eyed. She ignored him. A tree caught her eye, one that looked as if it had been severed halfway up at a jagged angle, with dark roots weaving down into the dank earth.

There. That's where she had to dig.

"Hey. Wait up!" Leif's voice seemed distant again.

Erskin carried on ignoring him – she had no

choice. Instead she ran to the tree and started digging between the roots.

Trapped. Must get out! HELP ME.

Her fingers brushed something warm and soft. Something living. She held her breath, and quickly scooped away the earth to reveal more of the buried thing. A small, round head, as bald as an egg apart from a few tiny, patchy feathers. A gnarled beak and bulging globes for eyes. A plump brown handful of a surprisingly warm, soft body. The moment she touched it she knew: *that's* what had spoken in her mind. Had that awful, suffocating feeling belonged to this ugly little bird too? She ought to be afraid of it. She really shouldn't touch – or go anywhere near it. But her heart went out to the little thing. How scared it must have been, all alone in the dark, thinking it would never see daylight again.

Just like she had been, clinging to the ridge of that chasm.

"A bird – underground? I've never heard of anything like it." Leif was squatting right beside Erskin, peering into the hole she'd made. She hadn't even heard him approach. "How on Yor did you know it was there, Erskin?"

Erskin didn't know how to answer that, so she didn't say anything. Leif didn't seem to expect a response anyway. He'd crouched down to study the bird more closely and frowned. It blinked back at them from Erskin's hand, drinking them in with its bulbous grey eyes. His nose wrinkled slightly at the gawky thing in her hands, yet he couldn't seem to stop staring. Erskin felt it too. Her first instinct had been to drop the creature in disgust – but somehow she was still here, holding it. Looking at it tugged on her heart, as if she were tethered to it. She couldn't bring herself to just abandon the little creature.

Trapped. Help me.

"I think it might be stuck," Erskin said, looking at Leif.

He rubbed his forehead. "I think you might be right. It would've flown off by now if it could."

Erskin was relieved that Leif had agreed with her, rather than asking how she knew. Feeling around its plump belly, she finally found its legs – one curled up neatly in its downy feathers, the other twisted. "Hang on." She felt further along. A knot of root had caught it at an angle. "Its leg is stuck." Erskin stared up into Leif's face.

"Can you get it free?"

"I think so. Here, can you hold its body while I try?"

Leif cupped the bird while Erskin's fingers worked

the root. Effort and concentration made her poke out her tongue. It felt like it was never going to give. Until suddenly the root snapped off in Erskin's hand and the whole thing unravelled, freeing the trapped limb.

"You did it!" Leif and Erskin shared a triumphant grin. Leif frowned and squinted at the bird. "But ... it's not flying away. I think maybe it's too badly hurt."

Erskin's heart sank. Taking great care, she scooped it out of Leif's hands again and held it as if it were the most delicate thing in the world. She could feel its little heartbeat tap-tapping against her fingertip; the pleasing weight of it in her cupped palms. In that moment she felt no fear – only pity, and wonder.

Its blue-rimmed, grey eyes were now squeezed tightly shut, and one of its legs hung down limp. But there was something in the air around the broken limb. Erskin blinked, and looked again, closer this time. They were golden wisps, floating like stray strands of broken spider silk – but only around the injured leg. And they were all knotted together. She frowned and glanced over at Leif, who narrowed his eyes and stared closer. "Wait. What are those ... threads?" So, he could see the golden wisps too. It wasn't just her. That was a relief.

Leif's forehead furrowed. "Poor little thing. It doesn't seem dangerous, does it. Just small, and sad."

He stroked its feathers lightly with the back of one dirt-encrusted finger, the swirl of soil etched into the lines of his fingerprint. "Is there anything we can do for it?" He glanced over at Erskin hopefully.

How she wished she could make *everything* right. Find her sister. Bring back Scrat. Heal this bird... The jumble of golden wisps gleamed and swayed a little. A shiver ran through Erskin's body as she watched them move. She had the sudden urge to touch them. Untangle them...

Her hands began to tingle. They felt hot and cold all at once.

The bird wriggled. *You can mend me. Use your luma.*

Was that the bird in her mind again? Its inner voice, speaking to hers? They weren't words, exactly – but since she'd heard its first distress call, interpreting its meaning seemed to be getting easier. But what on Yor was luma?

What do you mean? she tried projecting, but she got the same answer.

Use. Your. Luma.

Instinctively, Erskin moved her fingers carefully down to the twisted leg, the claw curled up like a furled fern, and accidentally brushed the golden knot of threads. The tingle in her hands redirected itself into her fingertips. One strand came loose from the others. She hooked it before it drifted away, and nudged it instead towards the bird's leg. With amazement, she watched it wrap around the leg like a gleaming bandage. The bird's leg twitched.

"Whoa," said Leif. "How did you do that?" But Erskin ignored his question. Now she felt certain she must untangle the rest. The hot-cold tingling feeling in her fingers became so intense it hurt, but she managed to pull the rest of the threads apart with ease and draw them one by one down to the bird's hurt limb.

The bird's leg twitched again. Its foot uncurled.

In an instant it had clambered to its feet in her palms, like a newborn chick fresh from the egg. Erskin's heart welled.

"It's about to fly off," hissed Leif. "It's OK!"

What's your wish?

It was the bird, speaking in Erskin's mind again. Her wish? The bird's weight shifted. It was getting ready to open its wings. Soon it would be gone.

Your wish.

Erskin squeezed her eyes tight shut.

I wish that Scrat… I wish he was alive. And Birgit… I wish for her to be safe from the dragon.

That was two wishes, but the words had just

tumbled straight out of her – and the bird turned its shining eye towards her as if it had heard. Then it pushed out of her hands and flew into the pale sky, up towards the sun. Its wings caught the light and shone. Now that it was in flight it looked majestic. Erskin and Leif watched it go in awe. Was this her doing? One minute its leg looked broken. The next...

"That was incredible," breathed Leif. "How did you do that?"

"I don't know. I didn't mean to, it just happened." She looked pleadingly at Leif, and held out her palms. "What's wrong with me?"

Leif stared at Erskin's hands. "I don't understand how it happened," he said slowly. "But you just helped something that needed helping. Can that really be wrong?"

"Everyone in the village would say so," she replied. "Magic *is* wrong, it's dangerous. Maybe I *am* hex-addled, just like they all say."

Leif snorted. "Listen, my dad's a sailor. He says that in every port he goes to people are afraid of something, but it's hardly ever the same thing. In some towns they've never even heard of hex magic – or they call it something else... And it's worth a lot of money. People are too quick to believe rumours, is what I'm saying."

Erskin couldn't believe anyone would pay to be hex-addled, but it was nice that Leif was trying to make her feel better. She let her hands fall in her lap. They had a speckled, almost silvery look about them. She opened and closed them, working out the remaining twinges and tingles. It seemed impossible, but could it be true? Had she healed the bird?

She looked up at Leif. She thought about telling him how the bird had communicated with her. The wishes. It felt like he might understand, that he wouldn't judge... But she didn't have the words, and besides, what would happen when they got home? It would only take him telling the wrong person – his sister Yasmin, for example – to convince everyone she was a witch. Anyway, Erskin knew such wishes were never answered. It was mountain magic, and that was not to be trusted.

"Come on. We've spent too long here already." Erskin got to her feet and had barely walked ten paces before something crunched under her feet. She lifted her foot to peer underneath.

Broken glass. What was it doing up here?

She looked around the clearing and saw more broken remnants.

Leif nudged a piece of it with his foot. "Hmm. That's strange," he said, and then he recoiled. "Ugh!

There's blood on this piece. And some here, too. Looks like..."

But it had already dawned on Erskin exactly what the broken thing was. It was a shattered glow lamp – the one Birgit had been clutching when the dragon swept her away.

13

WHEN ERSKIN LOOKED UP SHE SAW BROKEN branches. Something had fallen here, from a great height – Birgit's glow lamp alone would never have caused that much damage. Had the dragon dropped her sister here?

"Birgit!" Erskin called, the desperation squeezing her throat, making her voice come out all strange. She and Leif searched the whole clearing but found no sign of Birgit – only more pieces of broken glow lamp, and more blood. A lot of it.

What did this mean? Was Birgit OK? It was all too much. Erskin sunk to the floor and hugged her knees. Leif drew close beside her, fiddling with his fingers. He cleared his throat. "She might've just dropped the lamp," he said brightly. "And the blood could be – oh, I don't know..." He looked around at the clearing, as if searching it for ideas. "Maybe a creature stood on it?"

"But there's so much of it," stammered Erskin. "So much blood. What if Birgit's..."

"Well, she's not here." Leif frowned a little as he thought it through. "And dead people don't get up and walk off. Well. Not normally." He bit his lip, and it hit Erskin just as it must've struck Leif: that they didn't actually know what normal was, up on Mountainfell.

Erskin hugged her knees tighter. "What if the dragon dropped her and something came and took the ... the body away." Somehow Erskin felt OK about telling Leif her deepest fears. She'd never opened up this much to anyone before – except maybe to Scrat.

Leif chewed his cheek. "Hmm. I dunno. That's a big what if. Come on; let's keep going. We'll find her, probably. No, I'm sure we will."

Slowly, Erskin got to her feet again. Leif was right, of course. What other option was there? She had to believe there was still a chance to save Birgit ... and if she was hurt, bleeding, the situation could be even more desperate – and that meant they had to find her as soon as possible.

With no clear path through the misty marsh, Leif convinced Erskin that their best option was to climb the stronger-looking trees. "Remember," he said, grinning, "if in doubt, climb a tree."

Erskin forced a smile in return, and maybe he was right. A view from above might help them find their way. Erskin found the tallest, sturdiest specimen she could, with plenty of good footholds to get her started. Meanwhile Leif found one a little way across the marsh that he claimed was taller, and vowed to see her at the top.

The air was much fresher in the branches than down in the stagnant marsh below. It felt great to get a deep lungful. But Erskin couldn't believe what she saw when she looked back the way they'd come. The true vastness of the chasm where she and Leif had met – and where she'd lost her beloved Scrat – was clear from up here: a black line stretching far on both sides like a wide and monstrous mouth. Her heartache erupted again.

"Psst. Yoohoo!" Leif waved at her, and then pointed at his tree. "See?" he said. "Taller."

Erskin snorted – but Leif's ability to distract her from her woes was amazing. She mouthed the words, *No it's not*, before turning her attention to the landscape again. The shape of the chasm, and the drylands beyond that where she'd met the pack of fox-like creatures, looked strange from up high. It was like a long, thick tentacle reaching across the lower slopes. At its thickest, she saw something glint in the pale sunlight.

"Hey," Erskin called to Leif, pointing. "Do you see that?"

"Uh-huh," said Leif. "What *is* that?"

Erskin squinted. "Is it a river?"

"No, it's too straight."

He was right. Whatever it was tracked down the mountainside in a uniform line. "And look how dry everything is around it," Leif said.

It was true – the whole area did look barren. Erskin remembered the fox-like creatures' bone-thin legs and mangy fur. She'd thought then that it looked like they weren't getting enough to eat. Was the mountain sick? What would make all those plants die like that? It was certainly strange.

"Look. Over there." It was Leif's turn to point now, and something in his voice made Erskin pay attention. He was facing the opposite way to the chasm now. The trees petered out not far from where they were, and opened into a definite route up the next part of the mountainside. But right in the middle stood a house.

It was a rundown, thatched cabin next to an old, twisted tree. It looked abandoned, but for an ominous light that glowed at the windows. Inside, a shadow moved.

A shudder ran from Erskin's head to her feet. Who on Yor would live up here, all alone?

"If ever a house was haunted, it would be that one," said Leif, and Erskin nodded.

Her skin prickled. No one could live here – and if they did, they would be hex-addled. And dangerous.

"We'll sneak past using those rocks and bushes for cover," said Erskin, pointing at the rough land at the edge of the path. "It'll be more difficult, but at least that way we won't be seen." Even as she said it, another wave of cold prickles whooshed down her neck. She really didn't want to meet whoever lived there. All the villagers' talk of witches flooded her mind – of Sibella Sifsdotter, the Lordsson's own love, who'd disappeared up here after she turned bad. And she remembered the woman's voice telling her to leave, telling the fox-like creatures to chase her. The sting on her hand throbbed.

Still – if they wanted to reach the dragon's nest, what other option did they have? Passing the house was the only way.

The house looked even less inviting the closer they got. It was a neglected cabin made of logs, with a sunken roof and peeling walls. Streamers of a kind of wet algae-like weed hung from the eaves, and the old, bent tree that stood next to it looked spectral silhouetted against the sky. The light coming from inside it was unmistakable now. Perhaps from a candle or a lamp of some kind, because it flickered occasionally. Erskin was relieved when they could clamber deeper into the undergrowth, and further under cover – a cluster of raised rocks shielding them from view.

It had got colder. Mist hung around in patches. Erskin's teeth chattered as she and Leif crept through the undergrowth, keeping low. The air smelled eggy and awful, but at least the fog helped to hide them.

At a crouch, the pair crept forward with Erskin taking the lead, edging ever forwards. Peering over the ridge between them and the house, she could see how close they now were to the bushes that surrounded it. They looked as if they'd once been trimmed like a kind of hedge, but were now nothing more than a thatch of sticks – much like those they were pushing their way through now.

Something small flew past Erskin's face. A flash of bright colour at the corner of her eye. Erskin jerked back and glanced around, ready to swipe at whatever it was. The last thing she wanted was to get stung by an insect again. But what she discovered peeking out at her from behind the twigs was no insect.

It was a fish. A fish, floating in the air. Erskin stared. How was it even possible?

Erskin held her breath and froze. The fish drifted out from its hiding place, flapping its fins as though swimming in the air was the most natural thing in the world. It darted first one way and then the other, keeping one round, watchful eye locked on hers at all times.

A chill prickled Erskin's skin. This wasn't normal. It wasn't right. Had Leif seen it? Erskin didn't dare to move or call out to him in case it attacked. Who knew what else this unnatural creature could do besides swim in the air? Her lungs were bursting from holding her breath. She wished it wouldn't keep staring at her, that it would just *go away*. But it didn't. Instead, it drifted closer. Erskin winced. After a couple of passes, the fish swam right up to Erskin. It nibbled her on the nose.

The gentle nibble made Erskin jump, but of the two of them it was the fish who got the biggest shock. It darted away into mist and disappeared.

Curious now to see where it went, Erskin took a few steps forward. Her foot plunged into something cold, wet and slimy. "Ugh!" She pulled her waterlogged foot out of the bog.

"I think they're swimming over the marsh water,"

came Leif's voice next to her ear. "Unbelievable, isn't it?" His voice made Erskin jump again.

The surprise in Leif's eyes mirrored her own, but there was a touch of amazement glittering in them, too. "There's more over there," he whispered. "I want to see what they do. Stay still, or you'll frighten them."

"*Me*, frighten *them*?" hissed Erskin. Her insides were a jumble of confusion, but she did as Leif said anyway, and stayed still.

Three swimming together – long, small and silver ones this time – streaked past. They didn't *seem* like they would try to do her any harm, but she'd stay on her guard. Slowly, Erskin put out her hand and held it there. The fish came back to investigate, weaving around her outstretched arm and darting between her fingers. They had round, shiny eyes like the first one, theirs flecked with hypnotizing rainbow patterns. To stare into them reminded her of peering through one of the mesmerizing kaleidoscopes that you could sometimes buy at the market. Erskin stared in wonder.

Something about the fish made Erskin feel certain that they wanted to play. She turned her hand, slowly spreading out some fingers while bringing others together, all her thoughts of the strange, creepy house gone. The fish loved it – treading air until the last minute before whizzing through the closing gaps.

Beside her, Leif chuckled with delight, and Erskin found that she was beaming. Could these curious, playful creatures be "evil", and "wrong", as she and the whole village had thought? The whole idea of these fish being evil suddenly felt absurd.

"Whoa," said Leif, staring at the fish, his eyes sparkling with the light reflected from their scales.

Even more came swimming over to investigate them. Some round, flat and shiny like silver pennies. Others long, straight and brightly coloured. A bobbly eyed one with an elegant flowing tail like a bride's veil glided over too, clearly wanting to show off its frills. It was as if they'd all decided, collectively, that Erskin and Leif were safe.

A dull thump and clatter came from near by. Erskin peered over the rocks and undergrowth in time to see a shadow falling across the light from the window of the house – something or someone moving around inside. Leif gritted his teeth, watching. For one careless moment they had forgotten about it. How could they have let themselves get distracted? *Stupid*. There was a *thunk* followed by a slow creak – the unmistakable sound of a door, opening.

The fish suddenly changed. They became jumpy and flitted this way and that, fast. Some darted and dived towards the children's faces as if to chase them away, forcing them to pull back. The air seemed to thicken with fear – their own, but that of the fish, too. The one with the flowing tail made a hissing sound and swam at Erskin, baring sharp, razor-like teeth. Erskin and Leif drew closer together, just as a large, dark shape loomed over them.

A youngish woman in billowing dark clothes stood in the doorway. Her features were striking but severe, and her piercing dark eyes were fixed on the children. There was something strange about her eyes – as if she had bonfires raging behind them. She was a witch, most definitely.

Erskin shrank back and Leif grabbed her arm tight, fingers digging in.

"After all my warnings you still didn't turn back. How *dare* you come to the mountain after everything the village has done!"

Her voice was deep and seemed to resonate. She spoke the way gentry did – the wealthy merchants who sometimes came by sea to visit the Lordsson. It felt like facing the scariest teacher in school, but far worse.

Confusion and fear sent Erskin's mind totally blank. "We're sorry," she managed to rasp, glancing at Leif. "W-we don't mean any harm."

Leif, whose face had stretched into a mask of terror, nodded in eager agreement.

The witch let out a nasty laugh. "Harm? That's all you villagers ever do. You people always want more. More, more, more. You don't even care that you're destroying the mountain and killing everything that lives here as long as you get what you want. You'll take from Mountainfell until there's nothing left. But we aren't going to stand for it any more."

We? Was the witch just talking about herself, or...? Erskin glanced around, her neck prickling.

It was Leif who recovered himself enough to speak first. "W-we don't know what any of that means," he said in a small voice. "More of what? How is the village destroying—"

"Pathetic!" The witch threw her hands in the air as if she was going to hex them. Erskin and Leif shrank back, but no magic rushed at them, only angry words. "You're as useless as the other one, and she was unconscious. But I'll get to the bottom of all this regardless, you mark my words. You wouldn't still be up here if you weren't involved."

The other one? Did she mean Birgit?

"No – please," cried Erskin. "You've got it wrong. We've only come here for my sister. The dragon took her. If you know where Birgit is, please tell me." Erskin took a step forward, but cowered as the woman's cloak and hair billowed out around her again. Fish scattered in all directions.

"So what if the dragon took something precious from you," she hissed, the bonfires in her dark eyes flaring. "I'm glad, after what you people have done. Now you know how it feels."

"But I don't under—" began Erskin.

Golden sparks flashed off the woman's dark cloak and tumbling hair like static, so that the air around her began to glow. As Erskin and Leif watched she drew her hands together, and more sparks crackled between them. She arched her long fingers and the sparks fizzed like angry wasps. At the same time whispers whizzed through the air like daggers, just like those Erskin had heard on the mountain before. They definitely came from the witch – though the witch's lips didn't move at all.

I have them – two trespassers. Come!

"You'll tell me what you know, even if we have to drag it out of you..." she boomed out loud, this time. "And then we'll make you pay for everything you villagers have done."

From over the rocks and behind the witch, white beasts slunk out of hiding on silent paws. They were the shape of cats, but enormous, and they had giant, pointed ears and eyes the colour of green poison, which looked past the witch and fixed directly on them.

14

"THESE CHILDREN HAVE CROSSED INTO OUR territory," the witch said, and it was clear she was talking to the giant cats. "It's time to show the villagers that we won't tolerate their presence here any more." The woman pointed and the creatures responded, baring their long, sharp canines.

Erskin grabbed a handful of Leif's shirt. "Run!"

Sticks scratched and caught on their clothes, but they kept on going and didn't look back.

"You can run, but you can't escape," Erskin heard her call out behind them. "You're marked." A stab of pain in her hand made Erskin cry out, and the witch cackled as though she'd meant for it to happen. The skin around the sting was red and sore, but Erskin clenched her fist against the pain and drove herself forward to keep pace with Leif. "I can find you again whenever I want to," the witch went on behind them, louder still. "I've been watching you ever since you set foot out here. And the creatures answer to me now, even the greatest beast of them all – the cloud dragon!"

Leif stumbled but Erskin caught his arm and hoisted him back up. "Keep going," she cried, though her whole body felt numb with fear, even more since the mention of the dragon.

They could still hear the witch calling out, distant now. "These trespassers must be punished. Torkel, come! Help me deal with them."

A searing pain sliced into Erskin's skull. In response to the witch's words came a faint and far-off roar. The dragon.

The two children didn't stop. They ran until the house was obscured by the curve of the mountainside, ran until Erskin's lungs felt like they would explode. Huge boulders dotted the landscape as if they had been thrown by angry giants. Finally Erskin stumbled to a halt, Leif falling to his knees beside her. She panted for breath, terror clutching her insides. The witch had said she was marked. How would they escape? Where would they go?

The hairs on Erskin's arms stood up. She held her breath. There was no sound, no movement that caught Erskin's attention, but the whisper of something in her head – like a thought. She whipped round to stare at the boulders beside them. Two shining, poison-green eyes peered at them from the darkness between two rocks.

Erskin froze. Beside her, she felt Leif do the same.

The two big eyes stayed fixed upon them as the creature padded silently from the shadows. It was one of the giant wild cats that the witch had called. It had kept pace with them with ease, without them even noticing it once. Erskin could see now that its shaggy white fur was patterned with grey and black, and its great, pointed ears finished in black tufts. Its ears twitched, as though picking up the faintest sounds for miles around. Perhaps it could still hear the witch's voice, giving it instructions. Yet even now its oversized paws made no noise at all. How could such a big creature move in utter silence – hear over such great distances? It had to be hex magic. Even its mind made barely a whisper.

This was far larger – and healthier – than the scrawny fox-like creatures on the lower slopes that the witch had commanded. Its teeth were white and sharp.

"What ... is ... that?" Erskin whispered, catching her breath.

"I think ... it's some kind of lynx," panted Leif. "I

heard about them from my dad. Only this one's very big. And angry." He gulped.

Erskin and Leif used the rock to push themselves back onto their feet, then edged away from the huge beast, going as slowly – and as quickly – as they dared. It twitched its ears and moved towards them, its eyes never leaving theirs. A part of Erskin's mind was reaching out to it without her even meaning to, like she had done before.

But this creature didn't seem to hear her, or it just wasn't listening. Its mind remained steely, locked against her as the fox's had been. Every step it took towards them was slow, deliberate. Its eyes flashed: it must know it had them, that they couldn't escape. Sweat trickled down Erskin's back. She swallowed dryly and clutched Leif's hand tight.

"Let's just," said Leif, with forced calm, "back away slowly, so we don't startle it into making any sudden moves. And then, we run again."

Erskin wanted to say, why? What was the point? It had tracked them with ease. But then, they couldn't just give up. She'd rather die knowing she'd tried everything to reach Birgit.

There was a scuttling sound. Suddenly the earth and the giant rocks were crawling with spiders. The pit of Erskin's stomach lurched, because she knew what came next. And, just as she'd feared, an ear-splitting roar came from above, like thunder. The roar was much louder and closer than when the witch first called to it – frighteningly so. The lynx lifted its head. They looked up too – just in time to see a long, scaled coil of body, as translucent as snow at dusk, blot out the sky. It seemed to be scanning around, as though it hadn't yet seen them.

Another stab of pain sliced through Erskin's head. She fell forward with a cry. Leif caught her. "What?" he said, eyes wide with fear. "What is it?"

Erskin couldn't speak around the agony. Something was building inside her mind. Some pressure. It was like before, when the dragon had first appeared, only worse. Erskin feared that any moment her head would split. That that would be the end of her.

But just as the pain reached white-hotness, something gave. The pressure exploded, like a bursting dam. The release made Erskin gasp with relief, but now she clutched her head for a different reason – because, where once there had been only agony, words were now pouring through.

The humans must pay for what's been done as the Witch of the Mountain says. Corner them. Capture them. Do not let them escape.

Could this really be happening? Had Erskin

actually understood the thoughts of the cloud dragon? Leif shook her. "Erskin, talk to me. What's wrong? What's happening to you?"

"It's the cloud dragon," Erskin managed to say through the pain. "I can hear it. Its thoughts. Like – like I could with the bird."

"The bird?" Leif loosened his grip. "You heard its ... thoughts?" She was conscious that Leif was staring at her, though she couldn't focus on anything for long. The sudden rush from the dragon's mind was too overwhelming.

Erskin nodded, barely able to speak.

Leif looked up. "You mean, you can understand the dragon? What's it saying? Actually, don't answer that." Dread clouded his tone, and he gave her a hard nudge. "We have other problems."

He was right. The giant cat hadn't stopped advancing, and its unflinching stare seemed to Erskin to drill right into them. It took yet another step towards them. Was it hearing the cloud dragon too?

"Can you walk?" asked Leif through gritted teeth.

Erskin nodded, straightening again. "I think so."

"Then we need to start moving – as fast as possible," Leif said.

"I think you're right." They quickened their pace until they were almost running – only backwards,

Erskin holding on to Leif for support. Until they couldn't keep facing the wrong way any more if they didn't want to trip over or stumble into a boulder.

The moment Erskin turned her back on the giant cat she felt a burst come from its mind, like tensed muscles springing into action. At the same time a loud, grating scream came from its mouth, almost like a bird call but shockingly loud. There was no doubt: it was calling out to the cloud dragon.

"Run now?" asked Leif.

Erskin nodded. "Run!"

But another of the screeching cries rose up, this time from in front of them, stopping them dead in their tracks. Another came from the side. More of the glowing green eyes peered at them from the shadows, from all around. Erskin clamped her hands over her ears to block out the terrible screams, all joining together. All calling to the cloud dragon.

And the cloud dragon, responding with a roar, changed direction sharply and circled closer, its long shadow snaking over the ground where they stood.

15

MORE CATS EMERGED FROM UNDER STONES AND bushes. They were surrounded. Erskin's mind whirled. *What could they do?* She and Leif clung to each other. The creatures drew near – they were so close Erskin could smell their musty fur and the stench of their breath. The grey markings on their faces made it look like they were grinning.

One moved forward from the circling group – the one that had first emerged from between the stones. Its eyes seemed to flash with triumph as razor-sharp claws slipped out from inside its shaggy pads and pierced the earth.

Pain flashed in Erskin's head like lightning, but this time it quickly gave way to the cloud dragon's words. Or, at least, what her mind was somehow interpreting into words.

You've done well. Now leave them for me.

The beast who had approached retracted its claws and backed away, its head lowered. The whole time the creatures screeched and the cloud dragon roared in reply. It was descending on them. There was nothing they could do. And now, sensing their job was done, the rest of the giant cats began to slink back too.

"They're backing away," said Erskin, just as more creatures retreated and a route opened up ahead. "Go!" She pulled Leif with her. Whether or not Leif saw what she had straight away, he ran too, trusting her.

Cold gusts from above blew her hair into tangles, pushing the pair forwards. Erskin didn't dare look round – or up. If she did, she knew she would see the cloud dragon coming closer and closer.

"Not far to go," said Leif, gritting his teeth. He nodded up ahead, where there were trees, but first they had to cross an open plain. If only they could get under the cover of those trees, they would at least be protected from the jaws of the huge cloud dragon.

The cat-like creatures still yowled and screamed, their cries echoing louder than ever – though by some miracle they weren't chasing them any more. But Erskin wasn't thinking about that now. All that was on her mind was getting to safety.

Leif stumbled but Erskin held him fast. "Keep going," she panted. They were almost there. So close to the trees.

The ground shook, knocking the children off their feet. A coil of the cloud dragon's translucent, scaled body slammed against the earth in front of them, blocking their way. Cutting them off from the forest and all hope of escape. Leif cried out and Erskin scrambled to her knees. The cloud dragon, its muscular front claws dug deep into the earth, stared back at her.

It had them encircled in its snake-like body. It had them totally trapped.

16

THE CLOUD DRAGON'S BODY WAS AS THICK AS ERSKIN was tall and enclosed them both in a giant ring. It lifted its enormous head with a mane of pale, wispy, cloud-like fur, and bellowed at them. Erskin shielded her face against the gust of hot air, and the terrible, ear-piercing sound. Leif buried his face in the crook of his arm and rested it on Erskin's shoulder. She could just hear him muttering under his breath: "No, no, no..."

The cloud dragon shifted towards them on its front legs. The coil around them tightened. Erskin put her arms around Leif and guided them both back, away from the head of the advancing beast. Erskin's heartbeat drummed in her ears until she couldn't hear anything else. She stared into its shining black eyes until it felt like the rage in them would swallow her up and drown her. A rumble came from deep in the dragon's throat, that vibrated through the ground and up into Erskin's bones, as though she and the earth were one. Her head throbbed dully as the dragon's words came to her: *Witch of the Mountain, I have them.*

So the witch and the dragon finally had them trapped. Erskin squeezed Leif tighter. But even now, waiting to learn her fate, Erskin couldn't help but notice something. Behind the dragon's words was something else, she was sure of it. A sensation, like a constant, nagging ache. What was that? Barely understanding how, she pushed further into its mind. All she knew was that she was seeking out the source.

The cloud dragon lifted its leg to take another giant step forward, and blood splashed to the ground.

Erskin's eyes widened. It had a long cut between its claws that looked red and raw, with a shard of sharp, bloodied glass still wedged in it. The moment she saw it, she knew that's where the dragon's pain was coming from. That was the talon the cloud dragon had grabbed her sister with. And there'd been blood where they found the shattered glow lamp. She'd worried it had been Birgit's, but had it been the cloud dragon's? It could easily have crushed the lamp accidentally in those huge claws. There'd been so much blood – more than any human could spill and survive.

In spite of everything, relief swept through Erskin knowing it hadn't been Birgit's blood. That, for her sister at least, there was still hope.

"Is it nearly over yet?" asked Leif into her shoulder. "Is it going to eat us?"

Erskin shook her head and hugged Leif tighter. "Not yet," she said, her voice shaking. "Don't look."

The cloud dragon's head loomed even closer. It was very obviously angry. But Erskin knew, now, there was more to it than that. This creature was also in pain – like the bird had been. And then there was what the witch had said, something about the villagers harming the mountain. Erskin didn't know what any of that meant, but she knew the dragon must think they had done something terrible. And now they were going to be eaten alive for something they'd had no part in. Over a mistake.

Erskin was about to close her eyes too, but the scratching pain of the dragon nagged in her mind again as it put more weight on its claws. There, if she looked closer at the air around the cut, were the same writhing tangles of golden wisps that she and Leif had seen before – around the bird's broken limb.

You're hurt. If you'll let me, I might be able to help you. The tendrils of Erskin's mind reached out to the dragon's before she realized anything had happened, but touched nothing. Of course – it was so huge. She may as well have been an ant trying to speak to a foot.

Erskin and Leif backed as far away from the cloud dragon's front end as they could, until their backs touched the coil of its ever-shifting body. Its scaled flank felt impossibly smooth and warm as it slipped against Erskin's palm.

Leif dared to look up for the first time as they bumped into the dragon's body. He glanced around, swiftly. Noticing where they were, a sprig of hope seemed to grow in him. "We can still make it," he said, clutching Erskin's arm.

She stared into his wide eyes, his gaunt, bloodless face. "What?"

"On the count of three we'll climb over its body and head for the trees."

Erskin stared at him, then at the dragon's giant, looming face, and then back at Leif. She nodded uncertainly. All the blood felt as though it was draining into her feet, making her light-headed.

Leif set his jaw. "Get ready," he said, breathing fast. "One."

The dragon roared and took three paces closer. The coil of its body pushed against their backs. And as its skin pressed against Erskin's, her mind was suddenly swamped with the dragon's thoughts, its sensations. It was like before, but much stronger.

"Two," said Leif.

But Erskin had stopped paying attention. Beyond the rapid pounding of Erskin's own heartbeat came the mighty, thunderous pulse of another's. The laboured in-out huff of breath. That persistent sting of the cut on its claws. Erskin felt it as if it were her own and drew in a sharp breath. And then came more sensations – more, and more. Thoughts. Feelings. They struck her like shards of clean, clear ice that gradually dissolved into her mind – and that her mind translated into words she could understand.

Thieves! Why have the humans taken my egg? Give it back to me.

"Two and a half," said Leif, glancing anxiously at Erskin.

Taken aback, Erskin stared straight into the dragon's eyes. Egg? What was it talking about? She could see the egg in her mind's eye then, too: bright and pulsing white and gold, only just bigger than the size of a newborn child all swaddled in blankets. And she could feel the cloud dragon's yearning for it – the ache in its heart for missing it. It became an ache in her own heart too, just as she had felt the sting from the dragon's cut.

Leif gulped, then took a deep breath. "Thr—"

"Wait!" Erskin gripped Leif's arm, not taking her eyes off the cloud dragon's. But she could tell that Leif was staring at her, shocked. "I can't explain, but, let me try something." With purpose now, Erskin formed her reply and pushed it out of herself with all her might, through her arm, through her fingers, into the cloud dragon.

What egg? What do you mean? Please believe me, we didn't take it. We wouldn't.

Erskin felt her words fizzle away to nothing against the cloud dragon's scales. They hadn't reached it at all. It hadn't heard her.

"I need to get closer to it," she said. "To its head, I mean."

Leif opened his mouth but no sound came out.

"Trust me," she said. "Please. I think the dragon's lost something. I … might be able to talk to it."

Leif hesitated for a moment, then took a deep breath and nodded. "OK," he said. "I'm with you."

While Leif watched, Erskin took shaky steps away from the coil of the cloud dragon's body behind her, and towards its enormous, looming face. She had to concentrate hard just to make herself walk. The cloud dragon made a new sound: a low growl that rumbled out from deep inside its throat and sent tremors up Erskin's legs. A warning.

She knew the dragon could eat both of them in one go if it cared to, and it would be her fault for not running like Leif wanted. Yet still she made herself step closer, and reached her hand towards its flaring nostrils.

Please don't hurt me. I don't know what's happened to your egg. But I will help, if you'll let me, and so will Leif. Just, please don't hurt us.

The cloud dragon cocked its head as though it was listening to something far off. As though it had caught a whisper on the wind.

Erskin thought the words again. *We didn't take your egg. All I know is how much you miss it.* She held both her hands out in front of her now, palms up, so that it could see they were empty.

The dragon roared and Erskin trembled. If it had heard her, it didn't believe her. She had to try again.

She was close enough now to feel the hot breath blowing out from its nostrils, like bellows on a fire. So close to the giant mouth, and inside, no doubt, the huge, flesh-ripping teeth. But if she could just make herself reach out far enough…

Erskin stretched as far forward as she could, and focused her thoughts towards the cloud dragon with all her might. *Please, we didn't hurt your egg. We didn't come here to do anything bad like the witch thinks. We don't know anything about that. I just want my sister back.*

For a moment the cloud dragon held still, as if poised to pounce. Then it pushed itself forward by the tiniest fraction, and suddenly Erskin's hand was touching the bristles of its nose. It felt warm, just as its body had done. Among the tiny, coarse white hairs Erskin noticed a spattering of minute and delicate scales, all with the same mother-of-pearl sheen as its body. The little bumps of scales were impossibly smooth among the hairs, and as her fingertips slipped over them, they shimmered. *Beautiful.*

But she mustn't get distracted – unless she wanted it to be the last thing she ever did. Erskin thought harder than she ever had before, used all her effort to reach this giant mind.

This time she didn't bother with words, though. She pushed out with her feelings and spoke with them instead, the way the cloud dragon had.

She squeezed her eyes shut and sent the memory of Birgit being snatched away in its claws – the wrenching feeling that came with it. She sent the dragon the memory of setting foot on the mountain for the first time – her heartache at losing Scrat. She remembered helping the bird, its eye glinting as it flew away. Her wonder at seeing the flying fish, then her fear when the witch appeared. And then she thought, *We didn't know about your egg, or anything about people harming the mountain like the witch was saying. You have to believe us. But maybe we can help.*

The dragon threw back its head and roared with fury. Erskin would have run, driven on pure instinct, but terror made her forget she could actually do such a thing. It didn't believe her, that much was clear. It was angry – but also in pain.

The dragon finally finished its howl into the sky, and turned back to Erskin, bringing its head slowly, menacingly, in line with hers. Her legs shook and her whole body felt hollow. One strong breath from the cloud dragon felt like it might blow her away.

Let me look at you, the dragon seemed to say. *I'll know whether you're being truthful or whether you aren't...* It lowered its head again, and Erskin understood what it meant. Trembling, she lifted her hand and placed it again on the dragon.

The cloud dragon reached inside Erskin's mind. She knew because her whole body felt hot and cold all at once, zinged and crackled and sparked. It was like a meeting of light between them – pure energy. A feeling of calm settled over Erskin, like slipping under the softest, smoothest bedsheet that smelled of mountain air and sunshine. She saw into the cloud dragon, too. It felt like being let into a locked and secret room that exists in a totally different place, like a dream world. She sensed its noble nature, its love for its egg – and pain for its loss. That magic ran through to its very core, living as it did in a world of cloud, usually unconcerned by the happenings of the lands beneath it. She understood that the dragon – all dragons – could change to become male or female through the course of their lives. So, what should she call it? The words *I am they* hung in her mind.

The cloud dragon grunted, engulfing Erskin in moist, warm breath. It smelled like hay on a baking summer's day. That brought Erskin back to herself with a jolt. Just as the cloud dragon opened its mouth.

17

"ERSKIN! LOOK OUT!" LEIF MUST HAVE SEEN THE dragon's jaws opening and feared the worst. But Erskin had a connection with the dragon now. A bond. She knew they weren't going to eat her. Besides, she'd seen something Leif hadn't.

Their teeth were completely flat. Not the teeth of a flesh-eater at all – but of a vegetarian.

"It's OK," said Erskin. She laughed with relief. From the place inside her where the light had met the dragon's, joy bubbled up like a freshwater spring.

A string of grunts came from the dragon's throat. Were they … laughing, too? Their mouth opened wider and their head tilted back. The dragon's lips pulled back over the flat teeth, and they closed their eyes. Erskin felt sure the creature was smiling – also with relief. But then she felt the familiar twinge of pain, and their mind became frenzied again with the sting of it. The dragon tipped back their head and let out a long, sorrowful moan. Thoughts of the egg – the dragon's thoughts – rushed through Erskin like a crashing wave, along with the words, *My egg. Someone took my baby.*

I'm going to help you with that. We need to heal you first and then we'll find your baby, Erskin thought. *Or try, at least.* She moved down to their injured claw. The piece of glow lamp was wedged in the delicate skin between the scaly toes. The blood was thick and red and fell in drips. It must have really hurt. If she could get the dragon to spread their toes, she would be able to pull the glass out.

This might hurt, she thought. *But you have to trust me.* And she hoped the cloud dragon could hear her.

They really were massive claws, and very sharp. Even with the certainty of the bond she'd formed with the cloud dragon, she still felt wary of being so close to those talons. But she took a deep breath and tried to lift it.

The cloud dragon moaned – it must have been painful, and probably too stiff to move easily. How was she going to move it to get to the shard?

Leif appeared beside her. He took everything in:

the cut, and the fact that Erskin was trying to lift the dragon's claw. He looked petrified, but he didn't speak or ask any questions, just grabbed the claw that Erskin had been trying to lift. "One, two, three." They heaved together.

The cloud dragon moaned again and thrashed their tail. The ground shook as it thudded down.

I'm sorry! thought Erskin. But at least she could get down to the glass shard now. She grabbed it and pulled.

The cloud dragon roared, but Erskin had the glass. Such a tiny splinter to cause such a lot of pain, she thought. But there's no way the cloud dragon could have got this out without help. Now she put her hands over the open wound without touching it, and looked for the golden strands she'd spotted around it earlier. She found them again immediately and twirled them out of their tangle with her fingers just as she had with the bird, urging them back to the dragon. She closed her eyes in concentration and, when she opened them again, the wound had actually stopped bleeding already.

She sat back on the ground, exhausted. The whole experience had left her light-headed but relieved. It had been far more draining, and yet so much easier this time than with the bird. Now the healing process could begin properly. Then she remembered Leif, and her heart sank. He would've seen everything: that she'd helped the dragon with magic. But when she glanced at him, his face was solemn and awe-filled.

With as much energy as she could muster, Erskin squeezed out again from between the dragon's toes. "It's done," she said to Leif, still eyeing him nervously. He nodded. "You did it," he said. "You saved us." And a smile crept over his lips. Erskin couldn't help but beam back.

When Erskin turned, she found the dragon's face millimetres from her own. "Agh!" Although she now knew that the dragon wouldn't hurt them, it was still a shock to be snuck up on by such a gargantuan creature. Tentatively, she rested her hand on their nose. *I'm Erskin*, she thought. *And this is Leif.*

I am Torkel. When the cloud dragon spoke to her, she heard words again.

Please, Torkel. Where is my sister? Erskin bit her lip. She remembered the smashed glow lamp, the broken tree branches where she must have fallen, and involuntary tears prickled her eyes.

It was not my intention to drop her, said Torkel. *Her light shattered in my grasp and cut me. I let go. She was injured in the fall, but alive. I do not have*

her now. I could not reach her where she landed.
The dragon dipped their head. *I snatched her up
in anger when my egg was taken. Everything the
humans had already done, and then my egg, gone...
But causing pain doesn't heal pain. I remember that
now and I am sorry. I have been searching for her,
just as I am searching for my own child.*

Erskin felt a burst of the dragon's remorse, and
knew they really meant it. She took a deep breath and
steadied herself – at least Birgit was alive. And with
the dragon helping them now, they had an even better
chance of finding her. But she was puzzled about the
egg. Perhaps knowing more would help her get to the
bottom of all this. *What exactly happened to your
egg, Torkel?*

Torkel rolled their head and a sorrowful moan
escaped their giant throat.

"Erskin," hissed Leif, gripping her arm. "What's
going on?"

"It's OK. The dragon's explaining. I'm ... talking
to the dragon." A blush rose in Erskin's cheeks. What
would Leif think?

He looked at her with widening eyes. "Right now?
In your mind?"

Erskin nodded.

For a while Leif stared, as if taking it all in. Then

finally he said, "Well, keep going. Find out what you can."

It began when the mountain shook, Torkel said. *I was looking for food when the shaking started, but when I returned to the nest my egg was gone. Taken. My child. It is all to do with the true Beast of the Mountain – the one the humans keep here.* Torkel growled as they projected the words. *It has lived here unchallenged for far too long, and now it has my egg and the humans are to blame.*

Leif flinched. "What's the dragon saying now?" he asked out of the corner of his mouth.

Erskin frowned. She felt even more puzzled than before, and with tiredness washing over her after healing the dragon, it was even harder to follow. "Something to do with a Beast of the Mountain, kept here by humans." She and Leif shared a baffled look. To the dragon Erskin said, *Torkel, can you show us this beast? We don't know what you mean. We've never even heard of it before...* A shiver ran down Erskin's spine. A beast that even the dragon was afraid of? That sounded bad.

It hurts me to get too close. But I can show you from the air. Come. Torkel lowered their head.

"What's it doing *now*?" whispered Leif. "Erskin, what's going on?"

Erskin turned to Leif. Now she took him in properly he looked sweaty and windswept after their ordeal, with dirt on his face and his usually neat hair all ruffled. Erskin knew for a fact that she looked exactly the same, but who cared – they had more important things to think about.

She stared at him, wide-eyed. "The dragon's going to show us the beast," she said. "Leif, we're going to fly."

18

"ARE YOU SURE IT'S SAFE?" ASKED LEIF. HE STILL looked nervous of the giant dragon in front of them – Torkel – and who could blame him. There is a fear that's healthy to have around anything that could crush you without even trying, Erskin realized. As well as the instinct to run that any prey would have around a predator, no matter how friendly it was being. But at least Erskin could help with that last bit.

"The dragon's name is Torkel," said Erskin, and grinned. "They have flat teeth."

Leif gasped. "You mean ... the dragon doesn't eat meat?" He stared at Erskin, who nodded.

"Yep," Erskin said. "Carnivores have sharp teeth but herbivores don't."

Leif shook his head. "All this time, everyone's been wrong. The endless stories people told about the dragon being a flesh-eater … they were made up. It was just hearsay and gossip. All those people the Lordsson sacrificed to keep the dragon happy were sent here for nothing." Erskin nodded in agreement. She had to wonder what had happened to the sacrifices – fallen into chasms, or eaten by other creatures, perhaps?

Torkel grunted and rolled their head for them to climb on. The dragon was clearly getting impatient now, and so was Erskin. She felt uneasy about everything she'd heard. If only poor Scrat were here, she would've dug her hands into his soft fur for comfort. But he wasn't. Scrat was gone.

Without another word they clambered up onto the back of Torkel's neck using the soft fur of the dragon's mane to help, and then clung on. Where Erskin sat was a mixture of shorter shaggy fur and scales. She stroked them gently. The pale scales shimmered green-blue and sometimes pink, and it all felt so soft. Torkel's mane smelled like the turn of a clear day into a storm.

All of a sudden, Torkel shifted violently from side to side. For a split second Erskin thought she'd made a mistake – that Torkel didn't want them on their back after all and was trying to shake them off. But then she realized the dragon was only standing up. Getting ready to fly.

"TORKEL."

The booming cry came from the ground, and made Erskin's blood freeze. Oh, no... She recognized that voice. Erskin and Leif stared at each other with dread in their eyes. There, riding towards them on the back of one of the giant white cats, was the witch.

"Not her," Leif groaned in dismay. "When are we going to get a break?"

"Torkel," the witch boomed again. "Don't trust them! Do I have to remind you that they're from the very village that's killing our home – that's responsible for taking *your* child? They're part of all this and no different to the rest of them. They'll betray you, just like they *all* do."

Erskin heard Torkel's thoughts loud in her mind, even though they were directed at the witch. *No, these little ones mean no harm. I saw it when I looked into the girl's heart. They will help us, I believe it.*

The witch reared back on the giant cat in a flurry of dark cloaks. "No – stop. You don't know the villagers like I do. They're treacherous. Dangerous. They'll turn on you when you least expect it, Torkel."

"Erskin..." said Leif beside her ear, his voice wobbling with uncertainty. "What's going on? Can *everyone* hear this dragon except me?"

But Erskin didn't have time to explain before Torkel's gruff reply came, along with a burst of impatience from their mind that almost knocked her off the dragon's back.

Enough! I'll help drive the villagers off the mountain, just as we vowed to. But I won't harm their children again. This one's sister was lucky to survive.

"No exceptions, we said. No mercy," the witch retorted. "If you won't deal with them then *I* will."

Torkel grunted, and thought to Erskin, *She is too angry to listen. I'll take you to safety.* Once more, the dragon prepared to fly.

As they rose higher, the witch glared at Erskin through narrowed eyes. "You can't fool me as you've fooled Torkel," she hissed. "I'll get you for this." Golden sparks began to crackle through her hair and from her hands.

Erskin was about to protest, to try to explain, but the dragon lurched and so did her stomach, and the witch on her great cat fell right out of view.

"I think we'd better hold on," Leif said. "Tiiiiiiiiiight!" He wrapped his arms so firmly around Erskin's middle that he squeezed all the air out of her.

Erskin's stomach lurched again as they surged into the air. Leif might have been screaming – but Erskin couldn't tell through the rushing of air past her ears. And her own screaming, of course. But a pulse of energy came from Torkel, through her hands clenching the dragon's mane. She didn't need to interpret it into words: it was soothing, calming. *You are safe with me*, the words might have said. *Trust me.*

They rose so steeply into the sky that Erskin's ears popped. Peering through Torkel's flowing white mane, Erskin glimpsed the ground where they had been standing moments ago – now green and distant with a smattering of boulders that looked as small as pebbles. The rush of air from their take-off flattened the grass in waves, creating ripples and patterns like those on the surface of a pond. The witch was still down there on the back of the great creature, staring up at them, her arms now raised just as they had been when she'd called the cats.

Leif and Erskin shared a look of concern. "Torkel," Erskin whispered into the dragon's mane, projecting her thoughts at the same time. It helped, she found, to speak aloud while she did it. "That woman – your friend – what does she want with us?" Who knew if she wanted to capture them, or simply have them killed? "No mercy" is what she'd said. Erskin shook the thought away. "Why did she tell you not to trust us?"

Sibella is angry with the village for hurting the mountain, Torkel thought in reply. *And for stealing my egg.*

Erskin gasped. Sibella! So the woman *was* the Lordsson's former sweetheart. And she really *was* an evil witch. The rumours, the whole scandal, had been true.

Torkel went on. *After the tremor, after my egg was taken* – a rumble came from Torkel that vibrated through their body – *she and I vowed that we must drive all the humans out of our home. Without them here to feed the Beast of the Mountain, we hope to destroy it, too.*

"But how do you know who took your egg, Torkel?"

Sibella was there and saw it happen, while I was in the clouds – but she was too late to stop them. Torkel growled. *She is as devastated as I.*

None of this made sense to Erskin. What did Torkel mean about humans being here? The villagers were afraid of Mountainfell, and never came here. Sibella would know that herself, being from the village.

We must hurry to safety for now, Torkel thought. *The witch is enraged and will not let this go. I believe she fears you have turned me against her.*

They rose further and faster. The air whistled past, almost too quick for Erskin to breathe it. She could see the whole mountain now, from summit to base, and everything in between. There was the village too. It looked so tiny and insignificant in the valley below – so small it could disappear altogether. And school and everybody in it felt like something she'd never have to worry about again.

"Wow! Look at that," Leif shouted in her ear. She couldn't tell where he was looking, and he hadn't dared take his arms from around her waist in order to point, but Erskin scanned around anyway. Below them rose a forest that grew on the higher part of the mountain. It was like nothing Erskin had ever seen before. It was lush and green.

"It's *so* beautiful," gasped Leif. "Those trees must be ancient." He started reeling off facts about trees but Erskin wasn't listening. Her mind was drawn elsewhere.

What amazing creatures must live in that forest? It was starting to feel as though not everything she'd been told about the horrors of Mountainfell were true. For a start, the dragon was no flesh-eater. All the talk of the bones of the dragon's victims littering the nest must be made up, but everyone had believed the rumours all the same, unquestioningly – everyone including her. In fact, so much of this place wasn't as it had first appeared.

The dragon curled in the air, changing direction. Erskin and Leif had to cling on tight as the wind buffeted them. There was the witch's twisted home, sitting on the edge of the marsh, and below that the dry, crumbling rocks and crags and chasms. Where poor Scrat had fallen. Sorrow fluttered behind the cage of her ribs, remembering. But, compared to the lushness of the higher slopes, it was all so barren and sparse. Nothing grew there. Everything had died. And the sickness, or whatever it was, seemed to be spreading.

"Leif," she called over her shoulder. "Do you see that?"

Leif nodded gravely.

At the edges of the wasteland, all the trees and plant life were dying. It was as if the wasteland and the growing marsh were two blotches on a parchment, slowly extending – one too wet, the other too dry. Would the wastes and the marshes keep on spreading until they covered the whole mountain? Until everything was gone? And at the centre of the decay, something else glinted in the sun, catching her eye – something straight, and shining. The same thing they'd glimpsed from the treetops.

The children had no time to study it any more closely as Torkel rocketed up into the clouds before plunging down again towards the trees of the forest.

Erskin clenched her jaw as her stomach lurched. The thick, water-laden air of the clouds cooled her face and refreshed her senses only for a matter of seconds before they were plummeting down towards the earth once more.

They coasted low now, over the tops of the trees, so that the uppermost leaves were whisked off their branches and into the air to dance around them. Erskin breathed in, filling her lungs with the fresh, fragrant air. Her mind reeled with everything they'd just seen, but this one moment was like the best dream of her life. All thoughts of the sickness on the mountain, and of Sibella, were whisked away on the wind.

On Erskin's hand, the sting burned like a hot needle had been driven through it. Then they flew into something, and everything changed. It happened so quickly there was nothing they could do to avoid it. At first Erskin thought it was some sort of pollen, or even a swarm of insects – but it looked like a black cloud. Whatever it was filled her nose and mouth in a split second. It stung her eyes and burned her lungs.

Agony gripped Erskin's body from the inside out and all her joints locked: she couldn't move. She couldn't do anything except think of the pain. All the strength left her hands. She felt her fingers loosen on Torkel's mane, and at the same time, Leif's arms loosen around her. He groaned with pain, and Erskin knew that whatever was happening to her was also happening to her friend.

Hold on, she wanted to say. We have to hold on or we'll fall.

But the words wouldn't come out. Her throat tightened and panic clouded her thoughts.

Torkel roared. Erskin could feel the dragon's confused mind probing hers. *What has happened to you? What's the matter?*

But she didn't know. Something had hurt them – they'd breathed it in and now there was nothing but agony. What could the dragon do for them? There was nothing Torkel – or anyone – could do now. All at once her senses were flooded with the dragon's anger, and words projected not to her but far and wide: *SIBELLA. What have you done?*

"HELP!" It was Leif, behind her. A single, desperate cry – but who was there to help them? Leif let go.

With horror, Erskin watched him fall. Her own vision blurred to grey at the edges, and then to black. The cloud dragon's soft mane slipped through her fingers as though it had evaporated. Through her haze of pain, she watched Torkel sail away through the sky. She fell towards the trees, towards the earth, with her friend.

19

IT DIDN'T KILL ERSKIN WHEN SHE FELL INTO THE trees – or even when she slammed into the ground beside Leif. In fact, she didn't slam into it at all. What felt like strong arms caught her and carried her down gently. Except those arms weren't human. For now that's all she knew.

If she had been able to think of anything besides her own pain, she would have been surprised by all of this. Oddly, the fall didn't even seem to have injured them. But none of that mattered. Whatever that black cloud had been – whatever it was they'd breathed in, sent, no doubt, by Sibella – was going to kill them anyway. Now it would just take longer.

She couldn't even reach out with her mind to Torkel, who flew in frantic circles above them, unable to land through the trees. But the dragon's mind was locked in argument, and Erskin could hear a voice that seemed to be getting closer, Torkel answering.

Sibella.

Witch of the Mountain, you have gone too far. You have harmed innocent children. Tell me what you did. What spell was it?

Don't believe their lies, Torkel, came the witch's thoughts. *They've got something to do with the Beast. Why else would they be here?*

For the child's sister. The one I took in anger. Take back your spell, Sibella. Heal them now, or tell me what it was so that I may do it.

I can't, came Sibella's curt reply. *I ... haven't the power. What's done is done.*

The dragon's mind probed Erskin's again, desperately checking on her. *Little one. Tell me what happened.*

It hurt Erskin that she couldn't reply. That she had just made the most amazing connection with a cloud dragon, had promised to help them, and now she was going to die and break her promise, and worse than anything, that connection between them would be broken too.

Erskin gritted her teeth. No. Even if it was the last thing she ever did, she'd try to make that connection again. Someone had to know what had happened to them – even if she didn't fully understand it herself. With all her might, Erskin pushed her thoughts out of herself, and prayed they reached the cloud dragon. *Breathed the black cloud. Too much pain. Dying.*

It was easier just to remember those moments when the black cloud had appeared than to go on forming words, so she switched to doing that. And Torkel responded with a roar. Had Torkel actually heard her?

Erskin's throat tightened. It was an effort, now, simply to breathe, and Leif was struggling too. She was so sorry to have got him into this. This was her fault. She wished she could tell him how sorry she was. With all her strength she reached across to him and he did the same. Until finally, with the last of their effort, their fingers touched, and interlocked with one another's.

Torkel kept circling them, but now the dragon's cries grew louder and louder. Erskin scrunched her eyes closed tight and hoped it would be over soon.

Except something was now scratching Erskin's arm. She opened her eyes to see a beetle the size of her palm crawling up it, all glistening black shell and wiry legs, and long antennae twizzling grotesquely. Erskin shrieked, but she was too weak to shake it off, and as she watched, two more climbed on. All around them, they were burrowing up out of the earth – ten, twenty, more. The whole ground was moving with beetles, which crawled out of the soil and headed straight for them.

Beside her, Leif was also trying but failing to shake off the beetles. He shrieked, just like her, and tried to twist and writhe, but it was no use. Were the beetles going to finish them off? Did they sense that they were fading and had come to eat them once they had? Erskin's arm had at least ten beetles covering it now. And one of them lowered its head towards her flesh.

It's going to bite me, Erskin thought. It wants to eat me.

She braced herself for the bite, but it didn't come. Instead, a momentary relief from the pain where the beetle had touched her skin.

Wait. Were the beetles helping?

More of the beetles did the same. Through her blurred vision, Erskin could just about make out what looked like little suckers reaching down from their mouths, and where they pressed against her skin the pain inside eased.

They really were helping. They were sucking out the badness: whatever it was that was hurting them. Tears of relief rolled down her cheeks and she laughed. Leif looked at her – his expression baffled and terrified.

"It's OK." Erskin laughed. Her strength was returning. She could actually speak again – a little. "They're helping us."

Leif's eyes widened, and then he shut them. His whole body relaxed, and more beetles climbed up on to him.

Erskin could just about lift her head again now.

Torkel's roars became clearer. Every time the dragon roared more beetles dug their way out of the ground to help them. Erskin took deep breaths as the tightness around her chest left her, and every last bit of pain was soothed away. *You saved us*, she thought to Torkel and the beetles. *Thank you, thank you, thank you!*

The grass felt cool and a little damp against her palms, and a delicate breeze that rustled the leaves was like a soothing balm on her face. It was amazing to be able to feel nice things again. Softness and gentleness. Not just burning agony.

Although her head felt groggy and started spinning when she moved, Erskin was able to prop herself up on her elbows. The beetles were still at work, and she watched them – not with terror or disgust, this time, but fascination. Wherever they touched felt instantly soothed.

They seemed to know where the worst affected

parts were, too. Perhaps it was something to do with those weird spinning antennae of theirs, which helped locate the badness inside like the rods people once used to find water. Now that her arms and legs felt better, many clustered around Erskin's stomach, where a dull ache remained. But it wasn't long before they drew that out of her too.

And, as she watched, the beetles who had fed the most began to change. They started to glow – a deep, dark purple. Their shiny shells split down the middle and opened out to reveal fragile, iridescent wings. The glowing beetles took off and weaved shining trails in the sky.

Erskin lifted the last beetle onto her hand, raising it up so it could fly away more easily. *Thank you, little beetle.*

The beetle twirled its antennae at her and dipped forwards in what looked like a gallant bow. It fluttered off into the air with the rest, glowing purple.

Torkel and Sibella were still arguing, somewhere through the trees.

I don't understand, Sibella thought. *You would help them? After everything they've done? To the mountain? To you?*

They are not responsible, Sibella. I told you. Will you not trust me?

The children could sit up now. A sweep of darkness under Leif's eyes made him look like someone recovering from a terrible sickness – but Erskin guessed she looked the same. "I think we were poisoned by the witch," she said. "That black cloud appeared around us and then my whole body felt like it was burning from the inside out."

"It felt like knives," said Leif in agreement. "Like hot metal inside me. The beetles saved us."

The deep purple glow trails hung all around them still. The beetles were everywhere – some digging back down into the earth, others flying, yet more nestled in branches, pulsing with their dark light. It was thanks to them – and to Torkel – that they were alive. Overhead, the trees rustled in a breeze, and Torkel cried out to her.

I cannot get to you through the trees. Beware the witch – she is coming.

"What's the dragon saying?" asked Leif, turning to look at her. She realized she'd been looking up at the dragon as she listened.

"Torkel can't reach us down here," said Erskin. "But—"

"But I can," came a voice from beside them.

It was Sibella, the witch.

20

THEY MIGHT HAVE HAD THE CHANCE TO RUN IF THE woman wasn't already upon them, riding the giant white cat. The children flung their arms around one another as she slid down from her mount and strode towards them.

"You might have everyone else fooled," the witch said. "The cloud dragon, the beetles ... but not me. I don't believe you came to this place only for your sister."

Erskin gritted her teeth. "It doesn't matter what you believe. I *did*."

"Rubbish. Not a single soul followed *me* when I left the village." A cloud seemed to draw over her eyes, extinguishing the flame in them for a mere instant. Then her eyes flared brighter than ever, and sparks of gold started to crackle around her. The children drew even closer together. Above, the cloud dragon roared and circled, unable to land, unable to help...

"Prrow?"

Erskin froze. Was she imagining it? Or did she just hear what sounded like...

"Prrowww."

"Scrat?" The muffled sound came from behind the giant white beast that Sibella had ridden on to get here. Erskin stared as something black and shadow-like wove through the creature's legs, and touched noses with it, before strutting towards them.

There, between the children and the witch, the black shape plonked itself down and whisked its tail. "Prrroooowww!"

There sat a big round ball of black fluff, a little dirtier than normal, perhaps, with two round, amber eyes and a big tail that quivered with excitement. A wave of joy rolled over Erskin. She wasn't imagining things. It really, truly was him.

It was Scrat. He was all right – just as she'd wished when she'd healed the bird.

Erskin let out a cry of delight.

"No way..." gasped Leif.

The witch looked horrified. To Scrat she said, "No! Get away from those people. They're dangerous."

But Scrat didn't seem to be listening, and nor was

Erskin. She rushed forward and scooped Scrat up into her arms. He was filthy and cold and he smelled of earth, and his silver markings seemed to have moved again and become several long wavy stripes, but it was definitely him. "Oh, Scrat," said Erskin. "Thank Life, you're safe." Then she thought, *I'm so, so sorry.*

In answer, he kissed her nose with his and rubbed her with his cheek. *Best human, I find you.*

Erskin's mouth dropped open. She could actually *hear* Scrat's thoughts now too.

"Can I...?" asked Leif, drawing in close beside her. Erskin nodded.

Cautiously, Leif reached out a hand, laid it down gently against the soft, black fur, and stroked. "Prrow." Scrat didn't even open his eyes, but the silver stripes along his back rippled with pleasure. Erskin had never seen anything like that happen before. Leif beamed. "I'm Leif," he whispered. "It's nice to meet you, Scrat."

Erskin listened to Scrat's thoughts for a moment, and then a smile spread across her lips. "He says it's nice to meet you, too."

"You can hear Scrat's thoughts as well?" said Leif in a whisper. "Can you hear all the animals?"

Erskin nodded, turning pink. "I think, maybe I can," she replied.

The witch stared, aghast. "You too, Fluffkins?

You've been taken in as well?" She sounded far more uncertain than angry, now.

"Prrow."

"This is my cat," Erskin said, drawing her arms around him protectively as she glared at the witch. "Would you try to poison *him*, too?"

But Leif's eyebrows had knotted together, and he stared at Sibella. "Hang on," he said. "Did you just say … Fluffkins?"

When Sibella scowled in reply it was enough to make Leif shrink back. But then she looked at Scrat, and her expression clouded over with confusion and uncertainty again. "Yes. He's my cat. Fluffkins."

Scrat looked at them both in turn. "Mooooww," he said.

Erskin stroked his tail. "You mean … Scrat?" she said, looking from the woman to Leif, who was staring between all of them. Sibella seemed less of a threat now that she wasn't so angry, so Erskin went on with caution. "He came to us out of the blue. I thought he was a ship's cat. Although sometimes he disappears for days and days and…" A realization slowly dawned on Erskin – about exactly *where* Scrat probably came from and went back to for days on end.

Sibella stared at Erskin, but still pointed at Scrat. "No," she said. "This is Fluffkins."

"Fluffkins?" echoed Erskin and Leif together. Apart from anything else, Erskin could hardly comprehend that this witch – who'd followed them, terrorized them, almost *killed* them – would actually name a cat ... Fluffkins.

"But he does like to go a-wandering," she went on. "And..." She gaped for a moment, and then gasped. "Fluffkins, you hound." The witch strode closer. The children flinched, Erskin preparing to run, to shield her precious Scrat. But Scrat wriggled and writhed in her arms as if he wanted to be let down.

"No, Scrat!" But Erskin couldn't hold on to him any longer. Once on the ground he sauntered over to Sibella and began rubbing his cheek against her leg.

Got present. Will fetch, came the thoughts in Erskin's mind. Erskin wasn't sure what he meant, but they all watched him trot away with his tail bolt upright, out of sight behind the legs of the big cat that was still waiting close to Sibella.

Not once looking at the children, Sibella went on in a mumble. "I haven't seen him for an age, to tell the truth. I did suspect he might have gone fully wild, or off on an adventure, hunting airfisk. Never thought he'd go to the village, though." Her face turned sour. "But then he returned an hour or two ago looking like this, with a crag bat in his mouth, so I knew he'd been somewhere he shouldn't."

Erskin stared at Leif, who beamed. "Told you," he said. "Nine lives!"

Erskin smiled.

When Scrat reappeared, he had something in his mouth. "Moww," said Scrat, through his clenched jaw. "Moww, Moww, MOWWERGHEW." *Got present. For all you.*

Everyone stared at the cat, shocked by the sudden weird noise he was making. Scrat began to circle, still howling in that weird way. *See present! See!*

Then he lurched forward as though he was going to be sick. Automatically, they all drew back – even Sibella. But it wasn't sick that landed on the ground at their feet. It was an object of some sort, writhing in a puddle of drool.

Erskin and Leif stared in disgust. The thing was small and silver and, perhaps suddenly realizing it was momentarily free from the jaws of death, flapped wildly on the floor. For a second it rose up, floating in the air, before falling back down with a sad, wet slap.

The witch wrinkled her nose. "Not again, Fluffkins," she said with disgust. Then, to Erskin's surprise, she spoke directly to them. "First he comes back with a crag bat. Now an airfisk."

"Prroww," said Scrat. *Nice present. You pleased, I know.*

Erskin could see now that it was a fish, just like the ones she and Leif had come across near the witch's old cabin, the ones that swam in the air and that had darted through her fingers, playing. This one was clearly badly hurt, having been half chewed.

A twinge of sadness for the creature mingled with guilt inside Erskin. It had been her cat who'd done this, after all. *Oh, Scrat.* But he just sat down and started to lick his paw, pleased with himself for bringing them a gift. Perhaps Erskin could help it.

She knelt beside the fish, just like the first one she'd seen outside Sibella's home, its round eye staring up at the wide sky, reflecting what seemed like the whole world on its curved surface. And there were the golden threads hanging in the air around it.

Erskin felt Sibella's stare burning into the back of her neck, but she had to focus on the threads. Carefully she caught them, split them out of their tangle, and wove them back towards the creature. When she'd finished, the fish – an airfisk, Sibella had called it – thrashed a couple of times and rose into the air. For a second it looked stunned. And then, in a flash of silver, it darted away into the trees.

Oh no. Present gone, Scrat thought, gazing after it. But he soon returned to licking his paw.

Erskin sat back on the ground and rubbed her head. Suddenly she felt dizzy. First the dragon, now the airfisk – perhaps it had been too much for her.

Behind her, she heard Sibella's awestruck voice. "You … healed it," she said. "Such power…"

"Do you see now?" Erskin said, but it came out as a weak mumble. "We don't mean any harm." Her mind swam with confusion and tiredness. She tried to stand, but staggered. Leif caught her. She felt weaker than ever. The ground tilted beneath her.

"Whoa. Careful, Erskin," she heard Leif say. "I can't hold you."

Erskin tried to speak but her mouth felt numb. Everything went grey at the edges and closed in. The last thing she was aware of was a strong pair of hands sliding under her arms and hoisting her up – and Sibella's voice, saying, "She's used too much luma. She's fading," before she slipped beneath the grey.

Everything was dark. Erskin was falling. From all around came a rhythmic humming, growing ever louder as she tumbled deeper. Some sort of mechanical churning? Fear rose up in her throat at the sound until it filled her to the brim, though she didn't know why.

Although she couldn't explain it, Erskin didn't feel like herself. And it was as if she was enclosed in something.

Erskin was falling, falling, falling – until she wasn't. All was still and silent, but for the relentless sound of the machine. Bit by bit, the energy was draining from her, or whoever she was in this dream, as if it were a thread being pulled, as if she were being unwound. She was getting weaker. Fading. And she couldn't make it stop. She tried to cry out but found she didn't have words – in fact she no longer knew how to form them. She opened her mouth to scream, but nothing came out.

And then there was another dreaded sound. That of scraping, digging. Light flooded in, hurting her eyes. Through the ache of the brightness, she glimpsed a high ceiling, painted blue: some sort of underground chamber. White stars were painted on it, and at the centre, a large spiral symbol – like the faint weathered one she'd seen on the cairn. And then two huge hands, reaching in to grab her.

Erskin woke to the sound of her own cry to find soft, white fur at her back, and Leif's concerned face bearing down on her, trying to say something.

But his words faded and were lost to her as she slipped back into unconsciousness – this time grey and steady and dreamless.

21

ERSKIN SAT BOLT UPRIGHT. SCRAT – WHO MUST HAVE been lying on her chest – did a roly-poly down to her feet, where he settled down again. Sweat trickled down her back and her heart pounded. Perhaps she'd cried out, because Leif dropped the book he'd been reading and yelled in shock.

It gave her some relief to see him, but where on Yor were they? They seemed to be indoors, in a house Erskin didn't know. She was lying on a kind of straw-stuffed sofa – how was that possible? Her senses pitched and rolled; she felt woozy and disorientated. The memory of her strange and terrifying dream was still fresh in her mind. "What's going on? What happened to me?"

"Steady," said Leif, rushing over. "It's OK. You passed out after … after whatever it was you did to help the airfisk, untangling that weird golden stringy stuff. It's amazing how you do that, by the way." He grinned, then went on, "But after everything with Torkel, and then the poison, it was … maybe a step too far. You passed out."

"Did I?"

"It sounded like you were having nightmares on the way here," said Leif with concern. "Do you remember anything?"

"I—" Erskin rubbed her head, but the words to explain wouldn't come. Their journey here was a total blank, but the dream she'd had was clear. It had felt a little bit like when Torkel spoke in her mind. But everything she'd seen had been so jumbled, so hard to understand. She glanced around. "Where are we?"

"Right. I'll explain everything," Leif said, "but you need to stay calm. We—"

He was cut off by the door bursting open. A woman, dressed in dark, billowing clothes, marched in. Sibella – and she was holding a long, sharp knife. "What's going on in here?" she said. "Is she awake?"

Erskin screamed. She tried to scramble up, but Leif held her firmly. He put a hand up to Sibella as if to say *I've got this*. Erskin could barely hide her surprise.

"It's OK, Erskin," he said. "Listen to me. She's helping us. She brought us here to her cabin when you collapsed. We rode on the back of that big cat. She said she knew how to help you. I didn't know what else to do," he said, more quietly. "I didn't have much choice. But she was true to her word. She did some healing thingy on you and it worked. It wasn't the same way you did it, though. Actually..." Leif frowned, looking puzzled, and started fidgeting. "She pulled some of that golden thread out of, erm, out of my chest, to do it. Said she needed it for the spell. It was so strange, Erskin. And it really hurt."

Leif rubbed his chest and eyed Sibella, then whispered in Erskin's ear, "Whatever you did to heal the fish seems to have convinced her that we're OK. Plus, the dragon explained that you helped heal them, too – once she was finally ready to listen, that is. Boy, those two are scary when they argue. All that roaring and shouting! Anyway, I don't think she's a threat to us now that she knows we aren't trying to hurt the mountain, or Torkel. She's, er ... making us some soup."

"Soup?" Erskin yelled, louder than even she had expected. She could hardly believe her ears – but at least that explained the knife. "Leif," she hissed, "she tried to *poison* us."

In the doorway, Sibella straightened and cleared her throat, although she didn't meet Erskin's eye. She'd been watching them quietly throughout this whole exchange. "I did, yes. But it seems I've been wrong about you."

Erskin stared at Leif. She could still see the dark shadows beneath his eyes from their ordeal. They'd almost been killed. They would have been, if it hadn't been for Torkel and the beetles. A fierce heat sparked inside Erskin, and her face creased with contempt. "You've done enough," she spat. "We don't want your help."

The witch sighed. "I am truly sorry. I thought you were trying to hurt my darling Torkel. Tricking the dragon. But I've seen the way you use your luma now – highly impressive." There was that word again – the one Erskin had heard in the bird's mind. Luma.

But before Erskin could ask about it, Sibella went on, "And I see how many friends you have in this place already." She glanced down at Scrat. The cat padded up the bed to nuzzle Erskin's arm and headbutt her hand to make her stroke him. His soft fur, brushing against her palm, was relaxing, as was hearing his contented purrs and his little, inner voice. *Give me fuss. I want fuss. Fuss now.*

Life was pretty simple in the world of Scrat.

For the first time, Sibella met Erskin's gaze. "I promise I won't try to harm you again." She actually looked genuine. "The mountain is my home, and the creatures are my friends. I thought you were just like the other villagers who come here. I was doing what I thought had to be done to protect what I love."

"We *could* do with a proper meal," Leif murmured. "We'll need our strength if we're going to find your sister."

Erskin sighed – she didn't know what to think. Her head was still woozy, and it was true that she would be no help to anyone if she stayed like this. And Sibella had helped her after she collapsed, according to Leif. So, perhaps, they really could trust her.

Warily, Erskin studied Sibella. "Torkel said that my sister is lost somewhere up here, and that she's hurt. If you really want to make up for what you did, you'll help us find her."

Sibella drew herself up, and for a moment Erskin thought she'd gone too far. But rather than hex them again, Sibella said, "I already am, child. I've sent my wasps to patrol the area where she was last seen."

"You mean you saw her once already?" Erskin sat up straighter, then had to lean back from the dizziness.

Sibella huffed and placed her hands on her hips, the glinting chopping knife sticking in the air at an angle. "Yes, I found her, after the dragon dropped her when the lamp smashed and they cut their paw. I thought she was dead at first, but she was just unconscious. Torkel begged me to help her. They were so filled with remorse; they hadn't meant to harm her. But I told them not to be so soft, and I left her to her fate. The villagers deserve everything they get." Sibella curled her lip, but she breathed in through her nose and sounded calmer when she continued. "Then it occurred to me that she might tell me something useful if she woke, or else we could use her as a hostage to meet our demands." Sibella ignored Erskin's and Leif's looks of horror, and went on. "But when I came back, she was already gone."

"So, you had her, and you *lost* her?" Erskin's voice shook with anger. "Birgit's wandering around the mountain, probably injured, because of you." She felt sick.

"Don't you get clever with me." Sibella's dark eyes flared with light. Even in her own fury and concern for Birgit, Erskin couldn't help but shrink. "I said I'm looking, and so is Torkel. And, while you were unconscious, the dragon thinks they saw her heading for the upper slopes – and that's where I've sent my wasps."

Birgit! Erskin's heart leaped just as her stomach knotted. "How was she?" Erskin asked. "Did she look OK? Was she badly hurt?"

Sibella frowned and said darkly, "Impossible to say. But she was staggering. Clearly struggling, as anyone would be by now. And, of course, when she saw Torkel she took off again."

Erskin sat back and absent-mindedly buried her hand in Scrat's fur. At least Birgit had been seen and was alive – for now. That gave her some small hope.

"Anyway, I don't know if you've noticed, but we have far greater problems," the witch snapped. "The village has been destroying this place for years, and these new tremors are a sign that it's gone too far, taken too much luma. We must act before it's too late."

Erskin and Leif shared a glance. Something was playing on Erskin's mind.

"Um. What's luma?" she asked. "You said it when you were talking about what I did to help the fish as well. What did you mean? Wasn't what I did" – Erskin swallowed, barely able to say the word – "wasn't it magic?"

Leif nodded enthusiastically. "I keep reading it in your books too. It's mentioned all the time." Now Erskin looked she saw the stack of notebooks next to Leif. *The Mountain Creature Compendium,* read the spine of one, and *Mountain Botany*, read another. A third titled *Sibella's Spell Book* looked particularly full.

Sibella folded her arms and studied both Erskin and Leif. Then she said, "Everyone can do magic when they're exposed to luma."

"I'm sorry," Erskin replied, very slowly, and asked again, "but what exactly *is* 'luma'?"

"Luma is everything, here on Mountainfell. The luma crystals enrich the mountain soil, which feeds the trees, which feeds all of nature in this place. And when the birds and the insects and the creatures die, their luma returns to the mountain. It's a delicate cycle. A perfect balance. What's more, luma makes everything unique. It gives living things on the mountain their magic. It's amazing," Sibella said, smiling slightly, "what one can learn from a dragon, and a mountain."

"You mean – hex magic?" said Leif. "That's what it's called in the village."

"Luma suits it a great deal better," said Sibella. "Because of its glow, you see?"

Its glow? Erskin thought of the strange golden threads hanging in the air, like stray hairs blowing on the wind, first around the bird's leg, then around Torkel's wounded claw. And the fish.

Luma.

"But why can I do these things now when I couldn't before?" asked Erskin.

Sibella rolled her eyes. "Because you've been all over the mountain, of course. You've been absorbing it the *whole* time. Sucking it up through your little feet. This very house" – she jabbed towards the ground with her chopping knife – "is built on a luma line." Sibella actually seemed to be enjoying this. "I wouldn't be surprised if your magic starts manifesting more the longer you spend up here. And the higher you climb, the more luma there is, these days. Now that the lower slopes have been ravaged."

The thought of it all squeezed Erskin's chest. It was becoming difficult to breathe. "But, in the village, magic is—"

"You really care what those villagers think?" Sibella scowled. "Ha! They don't know a thing. There's nothing more natural than magic."

Leif shot upright. "Erskin, remember what I told you about my dad? He said he's been to places where they see magic differently – even to places where it's worth a lot of money..." But he stopped when he saw how crestfallen Erskin looked. Her mind was whirring; this was so different to everything she'd been told and had believed.

"Hey," he said as he nudged her shoulder with his. The warmth of it instantly relaxed her. "I don't know whether magic is right or wrong. That's not something I can get my head around, and anyway, I'm starting to think it's bigger than that, and maybe 'right' or 'wrong' isn't the best way to think about it." He shrugged. "Maybe it just kind of *is*."

The thoughts swam through Erskin's head: the connections she'd felt with Scrat and with other animals, which had been getting stronger and stronger, until now she could even understand the cloud dragon. This ability to heal things. None of it was normal, and yet ... was it really as wrong as all that? Her mind felt befuddled.

"Luma gives each person a gift. It brings out what's inside them," Sibella said, then muttered, "It doesn't make a jot of difference whether you like it or not."

"Hang on. What's your luma, then?" Leif asked Sibella, frowning. "You seem to be able to do a lot of things – not just one."

Sibella narrowed her eyes. "Sharp one, aren't you. My skill lies in the ability to steal. I can see the properties of different luma, take it, and use it in my spells. I roam this mountain collecting luma from every source I can – plants, animals, even people."

Leif gulped, and absently rubbed his chest. "So, when you helped Erskin..."

The witch smirked. "I stole some of your core luma, yes. Your life force. Just a pinch," she added when Leif's face dropped. "Too small an amount to harm you. Much."

Confusion and irritation were building in Erskin like a pressure behind her temples. Something Sibella had said was bothering her – about everyone having one gift. "But I have two." Sibella and Leif stared at her. "Two abilities," Erskin went on. "I can hear creatures' thoughts, and I can heal. Why?"

For a moment Sibella paused, then said in a quiet voice, "Healing is different. Healing is a skill that can be learned, but only when one is deeply in tune with the mountain. *Listening* to it, on some level. I have developed my own method, of course. But what *you* did..." Sibella paused, studying Erskin, and Erskin was sure she saw a flicker of jealousy pass over her face before she went on. "I've never seen anything quite like that."

"Humph," grumbled Erskin. "That can't be right. Listening isn't my strong point, apparently." Her head hurt, and she was getting hungry.

"There are different ways of listening," Sibella replied, "and different things to listen *to*, besides human beings and their petty business. A place might speak in the way its plant life blooms – or dies. It might even speak through thoughts and dreams."

Erskin frowned and looked away. All of this felt overwhelming.

For the first time, she took in their surroundings properly. Despite the cabin's shambolic look from the outside, the interior was warm and cosy; it looked much bigger from inside too.

Dried flowers and herbs hung in bunches from the ceiling, filling the whole place with a musty, flowery scent. There were makeshift bookshelves as well as a dressing mirror and curved-legged dressing table, cluttered with glinting glass bottles. They each had labels that said things like, *SIGHT OF TELLERHAWK*, *ESSENCE OF DEATHROOT* and *VOICE OF CRAG BAT*.

Those sounded a lot like potions, for making spells. Unease made Erskin shift around. But then something else caught her attention – there, half hidden among the bottles, was a photograph in a frame, with a small white flower tucked in at the edge. It was a picture of a handsome, young-ish man with a broad smile. Wait a minute. Was that...? Erskin stared harder. It was! It was Aleksander the Lordsson, she was sure of it, though it must have been taken some years ago. Leif followed her gaze.

When Sibella saw them looking, she slammed the picture face down. The children jumped and Scrat gave a grumbling mew.

Sibella glared at the children. The calmer Sibella, the one who'd been willing to explain things to them, was gone – her mood had flipped again. "These vegetables won't chop themselves," she boomed. "I'm not *that* powerful." And with that she turned and marched out of the room.

22

FOR A WHILE THE CHILDREN SAT IN STUNNED SILENCE.

"Why would Sibella have a picture of the Lordsson?" Erskin whispered to Leif. "She hates people. Especially the ones from the village."

Leif shrugged. "Witchcraft? She might be hexing him." He was clearly joking, but only half.

Erskin didn't think it was that, though. "Hm. They were *together* once, weren't they? Before, you know, it all turned into a big scandal when they discovered she was a witch."

Leif went on, serious this time. "Maybe it's to remember a time when things were better? I don't know. Grown-ups don't make sense."

Maybe Leif was right. Or maybe there was more to it. Erskin didn't know either. It was too much to think about, along with everything Sibella had revealed – about Birgit, about the mountain. About magic.

Erskin walked over to the dressing table, but decided not to touch the frame, or the white flower that was now lying on the tabletop. Instead, she investigated the glass bottles. Next to them were what looked like pages torn from a book. One read:

SPELL FOR TRACKING
With the voice of the queen wasp, mix sight of the tellerhawk.
Now the hive's eyes and tongue are yours. May their stings find your enemies and plague them with your thoughts.

There were more underneath:

SPELL TO CONTROL MINDS
Take dragonthought and focus to find your targets.
Grip hard once found and don't let go.

SPELL FOR HIDING
Weave the vanishing of wood foxes with silence sap.
Now you will be shrouded from probing minds and eyes.

And:

SPELL TO CREATE A POISON
Take essence of deathroot and scatter it to
the wind.
Your enemies must be in sight to strike
them down.

Erskin shuddered. "What do you make of all the things she's told us?" she said, chewing her lip. "Can all that stuff about luma be true?"

"Don't know," said Leif. "But I've been reading her books. Can you believe she let me? They're fascinating. Did you know she's been doing research up here? She's been recording *everything*. The bits I've read talk about this luma all the time. But they also talk about the luma being drained. They say *that's* what's killing the mountain – and that it's something to do with what the villagers are keeping here. She calls it Drell..."

Erskin nodded. "Torkel said something about the villagers keeping a big beast up here too. They said it was killing the mountain. Maybe Drell is its name..." Erskin rolled her shoulders and thought. She still felt weak after passing out. For some reason, a flash of her dream came back to her. The strange, rhythmic humming, the hands reaching towards her. It made her skin rise up in goosebumps. "But how can the *village* be responsible when no one ever comes here? Only those who've been lost. None of this makes sense."

"Maybe it's a monster that the villagers sent up here?" Leif said, wide-eyed.

Erskin shook her head. The villagers believed the monsters come from the mountain, not the other way around. She remembered the terrible blot on the mountainside that they'd glimpsed from Torkel's back before the poison cloud hit them – the way the land around it was dying. It pained her to think that all of the creatures she'd seen on this mountain could be in danger – and Torkel too. Even the thought of those lush green forests they'd seen on the higher slopes turning to marsh and drylands made her stomach turn. It was amazing how much her attitude towards the mountain had changed in such a short time. But she felt responsible for Mountainfell now, and if the villagers were somehow causing its destruction, she had to do something to stop it.

They ate around a table fashioned from a round, ringed tree trunk. Sibella was silent and her mood was dark as she ate – she must still have been angry from earlier. A shoal of the curious floating fish drifted in through an open window, but Sibella leaped up, grabbed a broom propped against the wall and started swatting at them. "Go on," she shouted, while Erskin and Leif ducked any stray blows. "Back to the Creeping Marsh with you! You are not to come in the house. How many times…"

Erskin and Leif shared a look, but, wrapped around Erskin's feet, Scrat didn't even bat an eyelid. He was clearly used to Sibella's outbursts.

"Blasted airfisk," Sibella grumbled, flumping back into her seat.

Erskin took a deep breath. It was time to be brave. "Sibella," she said. "Will you tell us about this … Drell … that's destroying the mountain? And what does it have to do with the village? If we can" – she eyed Leif for backup – "we want to help."

"You've been reading my books carefully," Sibella said, glancing at Leif. It was hard for Erskin to read her tone, but Leif looked up from his bowl and nodded so vigorously his soup nearly spilled.

"Erskin's right. We want to help," he said nervously. The tension caused by the photograph of the Lordsson earlier had made them all edgy.

Sibella studied them both, her spoon held in limbo between her mouth and her bowl. "Really?" she asked, narrowing her eyes. "You would really help us?"

Erskin nodded. "Torkel spoke of a beast kept here by humans. And Leif read about something called

'Drell' in your notebooks. Is that the beast's name? Is that what's hurting the mountain?"

Sibella sat back in her chair. "Yes, that's all true. Or at least that's Torkel's understanding. Drell is the human word. It's a machine built by the villagers, and it's draining all the luma from this place. Syphoning it off." She sighed. "The luma is being stripped out at an alarming rate, and that's harming the mountain. Some parts of the lower slopes are crumbling, and other parts are rotting. The Creeping Marsh never used to reach this close to my door... What's more, it's now causing these tremors. The ground is being weakened, and that's dangerous."

A machine? The strange, mechanical hum from Erskin's nightmare came back to her. "Why?" she asked. "What for?"

Sibella narrowed her eyes even further. "You mean you really don't know? I'd assumed everyone in the village was in on it by now. That's who I mistook you for, at first – fresh recruits, or at least *somehow* involved... But Aleksander and his father must still be keeping it secret from all but the workers."

Cutlery clattered and Erskin and Leif gaped. "Aleksander the Lordsson?" said Erskin. "*He's* the one responsible?" Surely not. He spent all his time maintaining the walls and warning everyone to stay away from Mountainfell – he was as frightened of it as anyone. Or at least ... that's how it had seemed.

After a glance at Erskin, Leif said, "Umm. Are you *sure*? I mean, how..."

Sibella's mouth drew into a long, thin line, as if she was trying hard not to show any emotion. It was a drastic change from the wild, raging Sibella they'd first met, yet her tone was still laced with something that felt deadly. "Yes, it's him. Yes, I am sure. And *how* I know is none of your business, before either of you asks that too. I believe he has his own ways of getting around the mountain – safe paths that he marks out. I think he sticks to secret tunnels though, mostly, for fear of the dragon."

Secret tunnels? Safe paths? Erskin thought of the cairn – of the faded swirl carved into it. In a flash she remembered where she'd seen something like it before: Aleksander's pin. His family crest that bore two joined spirals.

"No doubt," Sibella continued, "he sells the luma to aristocrats and nobles on the mainland with more money than integrity." She clenched her jaw.

"But why would anyone want that? Everyone knows that magic is..." Erskin was going to say that everyone knows magic is dangerous and bad. But she realized that even *she* wasn't so sure about that any more, and hadn't Leif said that there were places where magic was viewed very differently?

"Think of this, if you don't believe me," Sibella said. "The Lordsson is the only one who has the wealth and power to have such a thing designed. Think of the research alone that that would take."

Erskin's mind reeled as she remembered the scientists who had come from the mainland, who'd insisted on going to the mountain, and whose names were now carved on the wall that listed the missing. Had they really come to maintain and study the drell?

Leif himself looked deep in thought, until he mumbled, "Maybe it really is just Lofotby that thinks magic is bad."

Sibella nodded. "Exactly. Imagine how much someone might pay for bottled magic, if they realized its true potential to draw out one's abilities. Whether that's hearing creatures' thoughts, like this one" – she jutted her chin at Erskin – "or stealing luma, like me."

In his chair, Leif shifted a little and stared into his soup. He seemed to be building up to asking something, but Erskin's attention was drawn to the dressing table at the other end of the long room – where potion bottles glinted, and the framed picture of the Lordsson remained face down.

"If you know it's the Lordsson," asked Erskin,

carefully, "why haven't you stopped him?"

Sibella glared, but her expression soon turned to one of hopelessness. "I've tried," she said. "Most of the drell is deep underground. Some access tunnels are hidden, others are hard to reach."

"Couldn't the creatures get to it?" Leif asked, perking up. "I mean... You can control them, can't you?"

"No," boomed Sibella. "The drell drains their luma, weakens them, so they stay away. Torkel allowed me to take some of their luma, and that is how I can speak with the creatures. But my power over them has limits. I cannot force them to go against their nature. They're wild, after all. Not *pets*."

Shrinking in his seat, Leif sucked in his lips and said no more.

"It's too dangerous to get to the drell through the lower slopes from here, anyway, now that the tremors have widened the chasms lower down," Sibella continued. "But there might be a way in for you through the natural caves higher up – beyond the Enchanted Forest on the upper slopes."

The Enchanted Forest? Erskin's neck prickled. The tales of evil trees conspiring to trick and trap anyone foolish enough to enter the forest flooded her mind. It was said they could move on their own. The stories had been wrong before, but even Sibella seemed wary.

Sibella sighed. "There's a bigger problem, however. As I said, the drell drains luma. It hurts Torkel so much that they can't go near it without becoming sick. Dragons are such magical beings that luma is in their blood, knitted into their very bones. And" – her eyebrows drew together and she sighed again – "as I took some of the dragon's luma, long ago, it hurts me to get too close to the drell now too. I had no idea that would be the price."

She studied her open hands, her knuckles, then balled them into fists. It struck Erskin how painful it must be for someone as strong as Sibella to feel so powerless to stop the drell from destroying all she loves.

The witch continued, "Until now, the dragon has kept to their nest and not interfered, as is a dragon's way. They believe that matters of the material world will work out on their own, given time. Infuriating, if you ask me. But, after the tremor, after Torkel's egg was taken, they finally saw that we had to do *something*." Laying her palms on the table, Sibella leaned towards the children, and her voice grew louder. "Finally, they agreed to help me drive out every human that sets foot on the mountain – abandoning the drell, leaving it to die, to rust. And to show the village that hurting Mountainfell means facing a *dragon*."

Leif and Erskin leaned back – Sibella was getting quite frightening again.

"But that plan" – she sank back – "hasn't worked as well as I'd hoped." She eyed the children, and almost looked sheepish.

Outside, distant, the dragon roared, and Erskin could hear the sorrow in them – the yearning for their egg. *My child, my Torkelchild*, the dragon called. *Where are you?*

Sibella must have heard them too, because she looked pained to hear their cry.

Leif eyed them both. "What is it? Is the dragon saying something?"

"They miss their egg," said Erskin, and she and Leif shared a sorrowful glance. But as her mind wandered, something struck her. "Sibella," she began. "Can Torkel actually speak to their egg, the way they can speak to us, and the other creatures?"

"Why of course," answered Sibella. "Inside is a living creature. Though it is just a baby, naturally. That's the worst thing. Since the egg disappeared, Torkel hasn't heard their baby at all. This is why we think the egg *must* have been taken by those who maintain the drell. The drell could be blocking their connection. That, or…" She didn't finish her train of thought, but said instead, "If the egg is at the drell site it will be very sick. In pain. Its luma will be being drained, and who knows what the Lordsson might do with it, if he gets his hands on it. Sell it whole, or drain its luma first – both would be equally barbaric.

But then, he would only see it for its luma. We must get it back, and we must stop the drell once and for all." Sibella looked away, and outside the dragon roared again.

Thoughts sprinted through Erskin's mind. It was true that the Lordsson did travel to the mainland a lot ... it was one of the things her mam always commented on. Though no one knew exactly what he did there, or who he met. He could've been selling luma, all along.

"Why would the Lordsson use luma this way, though? How does he even know it exists?" said Erskin, as much to herself as anything.

"Why do you think?" Sibella snapped. "Wealth. That's all his Lord father cares about, and all Aleksander cares about is proving himself to that wretched man. He tasked Aleksander with draining more and more luma to show that he has what it takes to be Lord."

The children paused to absorb this and waited for Sibella to answer Erskin's second question – about how the Lordsson knew about luma. But the witch let the silence linger.

The children shared a glance. Erskin knew from Leif's eyes that he was thinking about the framed picture too. Why did Sibella have it, when she thought Aleksander was behind all this?

"Um. Sibella?" said Erskin, glancing again at the dressing table.

Suddenly the witch became very interested in her soup. "Mm, delicious," she said into the silence. "It's the mattoos that make it. These will be the best mattoos you've ever tasted, I guarantee. Bursting with luma." She clearly didn't want to talk about Aleksander any more.

After a long silence, Leif wrinkled his nose. "So," he said, changing the subject, "there is still luma on the mountain? The drell hasn't taken it all."

"The drell still hasn't reached all the luma that's higher up. Though it will, eventually," Sibella said. "But it's still there. It's still powerful enough to affect two little things like you who are used to that dried-up old village." She raised an eyebrow.

Again, Leif looked thoughtful – but an idea struck Erskin before he could speak. "Wait a minute!"

They both looked at her.

"If Leif and I have been exposed to less luma, does that mean the drell won't hurt us the way it hurts you? It doesn't hurt Aleksander, or the workers, does it? And they must have some luma too, if they've been on the mountain."

Sibella frowned. "True," she said slowly. "It won't make you sick, as it does Torkel and I. But it will likely still affect your power. Drain your magic, as it does the plants and creatures. If you get too close while it's still working, your magic will be weaker."

"Even so," Erskin went on, "if we could just find a way in – maybe through these tunnels – we might be able to shut it down for good." Plus, that would take them close to the Enchanted Forest, near to the upper slopes where Torkel had last seen Birgit.

Sibella's eyes lit up, this time not with raging bonfires – but with fireworks. "Maybe you two aren't so useless, after all," she said, raising an eyebrow. "This place has been calling for someone to heal it for some time. Who would have thought that those people would be ... *you*." She looked the children up and down, and not in an entirely pleasant way. "But the mountain knows what it needs, and usually finds a way to get it too. All this time I thought it was me the mountain needed. That *I* was the one it called. But perhaps..." Sibella gazed out of the window with a small frown. More airfisk had gathered there, investigating the glass and making shocked-looking "o"s with their little mouths as they edged closer to the opening. But Sibella stared right past them this time, and didn't seem to notice.

All of them were silent as they took in Sibella's words. Only the sound of Scrat's snores from under the table broke the peace.

23

As soon as they'd finished their soup, Erskin dragged Leif outside to make their plan. The old tree looked less threatening than when they'd first seen it. It had a short, fat trunk and seemed to split in two at the top, as if it had once been struck by lightning. The niche it had made looked perfect for sitting in. They both clambered up.

"Right," Erskin began as soon as they'd settled into the tree, "we should make a proper plan." She tried to sound confident, but her mind was whirring. Could they really stop the drell? Who knew how dangerous it would be? And what of the Lordsson – would he try to stop them somehow? It sounded like he'd never give up on his machine. It was his chance to prove he could one day be Lord, and anyone could see what that meant to Aleksander by the way he strutted around the village and wore his family crest so proudly.

She remembered how he'd stood in front of the whole village after the tremor and lied so easily. He'd been lying – or at least, not telling them the whole truth – for years. So, what would he be prepared to do to her and Leif, if they got in the way?

Fear made her stomach twist. Even having Scrat snuggled around her shoulders didn't bring any comfort. But she had no choice. Yes, Mountainfell was dangerous and wild, but it was also wondrous, and special, and home to so much innocent life. She had to do what she could to protect it.

Torkel's egg was somewhere all alone, too – perhaps missing its parent as much as Torkel missed their baby. The same way Erskin missed her sister. Birgit was still up here, in the Enchanted Forest somewhere, and she couldn't leave without her. It pained her to think that Birgit was out on the mountain, injured and alone.

Erskin blinked, coming back to herself. She glanced at Leif. "Er, Leif? Are you ... hugging the tree?"

Leif, nestled on one side with his arms wrapped around one of the tree's two largest branches, looked up. "No!" His cheeks went rose-red. "Well, yeah. Sort of. I just like them, you know? They feel all warm. You can tell they're alive, can't you?"

Erskin smiled; his enthusiasm was infectious. She hadn't really thought about trees as *living*, like Scrat, or the creatures of the mountain. But Leif was right, of course. She ran her hand over the rough bark of the branch on her side of the niche. It did feel warm. More than warm: alive.

"I wonder what trees think about," Leif said.

Erskin sighed, but she could hardly be annoyed with Leif for getting distracted. That was her speciality. And it was nice to hear him talk about the things he loved. Mountainfell really was full of wonders.

Leif went on, "I wonder what they would say to us if they *could* talk. Did you know they speak to each other? They're connected by an underground network of fungi. And if a tree is sick, the others in its network share their nutrients, to help it get better. I read about that in Sibella's book just now. But ... you're probably not interested." Leif rubbed the back of his neck and looked sideways.

"Why wouldn't I be?"

"It's OK if you're not," Leif said, blushing even deeper. "I know most people think it's weird to even care."

"I don't." Erskin forced a smile, but sighed again.

"What's up?" said Leif, shifting towards her.

"Oh, I don't know," said Erskin – but that was

a lie. Leif deserved a better explanation, so she tried again. "I wish people could like whatever they like and just – be themselves, without being called weird for it. You talk to trees, and you ask a *billion* questions about the stuff that interests you – but it means a lot to you and you should be able to do what makes you happy. You think for yourself. I feel so *different* to other people too, like I don't fit in at the village. I never have. I don't think like them, and I don't act like them. But I just don't know any other way to *be*." She looked away. It had all come out in a horrible, embarrassing blurt.

Leif didn't answer immediately. He sat back and thought in his ponderous way. They both looked up at the two moons, already hanging overhead. Pink and violet streaked across the sky as the sun set for eventide and the birds sang to each other. Erskin wondered if one of the voices among them was the bird she'd helped that day. What would have happened to it if she hadn't been there – if she hadn't set it free? And then there was her wish. Scrat had come back... Did that mean Birgit would be OK too?

"Don't, then," said Leif finally.

Erskin frowned. "Don't what?"

"Don't try to fit in." He turned to her with his chin raised. "We can be different together."

It felt as though something had broken inside her, and all the bad thoughts and feelings she'd bottled up for as long as she could remember flowed out of her and into the clear sky. It felt good, letting it go – until she realized she had bigger problems. "Oh, Leif," she said. "I hadn't even thought. The villagers are going to get the shock of their lives when I turn up with magic, aren't they?" What if they refused to even let her live there any more?

Leif shrugged. "They'll just have to deal with it. You can talk to creatures. Heal them, too. You can't wish that away just because of the villagers, Erskin. I'd..." He paused and then went on more quietly, "I'd love to have something... But what have I got? Nothing." He looked so sad, tracing the tree's bark with his finger.

Erskin stared at him with her mouth open. "Are you – actually wishing you had magic?"

"Hmm." Leif rubbed the back of his neck. "I sort of am. Yeah. I mean, am I going to be the only human exposed to luma to have no magic at all?"

Erskin stifled a laugh. This felt strange. She'd spent so long being afraid of the mountain and its power, and wishing to be just like everyone else – not a weird "hex-addled" outer-edge dweller. And now, here she was, talking about having magic, and although she was still afraid of what people would think, the truth was, she liked what she could do. She could understand why Leif would want magic too.

Leif turned to her with a mock-pout on his face.

"It must be something," Erskin said, trying to be helpful. "Maybe your magic is, I don't know... Knowing a lot from books."

"*Knowing a lot from books,*" Leif repeated, pulling a face of utter disgust. "Knowing. A lot. From. Books. That is *not* magic."

"It's not far off."

"Stop, Erskin. Just stop. No. I'm talking about things like levitation here. Mind control. You know. *Proper magic.*"

It was impossible for Erskin to contain her laughter now.

Leif seemed so thrilled to have entertained her that he practically bounced. "You can laugh," he shrilled with a huge, satisfied grin plastered over his face. "But I'm telling you now, if my magic power is having *no* magic power at all, I'm going to—" He stopped, because at that very moment the ground began to shake. A rumble that grew more violent by the second, until the tree they sat in creaked and groaned, and she and Leif were clinging on so they weren't hurled out.

Scrat screeched, shot into Erskin's arms and shivered there. *Scrat not like. Scrat not like.*

Erskin and Leif stared at each other. It was another tremor – even more violent than before.

The long, translucent body of the cloud dragon appeared above the cabin roof, blotting out the moons. Torkel twisted in the sky, like a worm plucked from the soil as the ground shook, and roared an ear-piercing roar. Then Sibella was at the door looking almost as pale as the cloud dragon. "The mountain is splitting. Come inside, now," she hissed. "Both of you."

24

ALL AROUND THEM, THE WILDERNESS CAME ALIVE with inhuman cries, howls and snarls while the cloud dragon circled and roared. A hundred voices clamoured inside Erskin's head at once, along with waves of sensation: panic, fear and dread.

The beast – it's stirring again!

My home, my child...

What's happening? Will it ever end?

Sibella was flung to the floor by the violent shaking. It was all Erskin and Leif could do not to fall from their tree. It felt like the tremors lasted for ever this time – until finally they stopped. Just as they did, the cloud dragon's shadow passed over them in a wave as they sliced through the sky. *Erskin, Leif,* came Torkel's gentle voice. *Witch of the Mountain. Are you all safe?*

That's when Erskin remembered that Sibella had been thrown to the ground. She clambered to her feet. "Sibella! Are you—"

But to Erskin's relief, Sibella was picking herself up too. "I'm fine. Just shaken," she said, dusting herself down, though the witch had a streak of blood down her face where she must have hit her head.

"That's the third tremor in a day," said Leif, his voice unsteady. "And they're getting worse and worse."

Erskin set her jaw. "We have to do something right away. If we don't stop the drelling that's causing all this, who will? Plus, my sister is still out there on her own." She tried not to focus on the tug of fear inside her, telling her she was too small, too weak, too insignificant to even try. Or the nagging questions. How would they stop the drell? And if Birgit was alive, would she ever forgive Erskin for putting her through this?

To Sibella and Torkel, she said, "This opening you found that leads to the drell – the one near the Enchanted Forest. Can you point us in the right direction?"

I shall do better, came Torkel's thoughts, and at the same time the dragon's roar echoed across the mountainside. *I can carry you on my back as far as the forest.*

There was no time to lose. Indoors, Erskin and Leif set about packing as Sibella piled everything they might need onto her dining table: food and water; blankets they could use for shelter and bedding; dry wood for making a fire. They would have to go higher still to reach the Enchanted Forest, and Sibella said it was a long trek. Torkel couldn't take them closer to the drell because of the pain it caused them – and nor could they land in the forest, because of the thick tree cover.

"The forest is wild, unpredictable," Sibella said. "You must be careful."

Erskin imagined tangles of thorny branches closing in all around them, and felt sick. But Leif, on the other hand, looked like he was secretly delighted.

While Sibella and Leif carried their bags outside, Erskin caught sight of the picture of the Lordsson again, which still lay face down on the dressing table. Still wondering what it meant, Erskin turned the frame upright. It was dusty, and the glass was now cracked from where Sibella had slammed it down, but the face that stared out from behind it was definitely the Lordsson.

Erskin reached for the small white flower that now lay on the tabletop to tuck it back into the frame. She had seen patches of it growing on the mountainside. This one gleamed a little, and still looked just as fresh as it had done yesterday. Surely it ought to be wilting by now...

As Erskin's fingers touched the flower, a bright light engulfed everything. Erskin reeled, disorientated. When the light faded, she was down by the wall around Lofotby on a clear, spring-like day, watching two people sneak across. Erskin gasped – it was Sibella and the Lordsson, but when they were younger. This had to be a vision of the past.

Once they were on the mountain side of the wall, the younger Sibella grabbed Aleksander's hand, but the Lordsson hesitated. "If my father finds out about us coming here..." Worry and uncertainty played across his face. "He already thinks I'm not fit to be Lord. That I'm too weak to make the tough decisions. If he discovers I've been breaking his rules, coming to this dangerous place..."

"Oh, who cares what your father thinks?" said Sibella, tossing her hair over her shoulder. "Nothing you do will ever make a man like that happy, mark my words."

Aleksander's shoulders sagged. "Don't say that, my love. People change. I'm not the child I was – scared and upset all the time after mother died, my head stuck in the clouds. I just need a chance to prove it to him, that's all."

"You needed comfort. Not discipline," Sibella growled.

"I know you don't see eye to eye, but he really is a great man," said the Lordsson.

Sibella scoffed. "He wants you to *be* him, Aleksander. You can't do that, because you're *you* – so stop trying. Anyway, look around. This is what you'd miss if he had his way. Isn't it beautiful?"

Aleksander gave a smile. "Yes," he said. "It is."

Time seemed to speed up. Erskin saw the pair climb across the wall again and again. Spring turned to summer, turned to autumn. Erskin's head spun. Just as she thought it would never stop, she was looking at Sibella's house – except it was only half built, and the Lordsson was building it … with magic. The house assembled as if on its own, but it was Aleksander who was conducting it.

"Our special place, where we can always come," said Sibella, turning to him with a smile. "Thanks to you and your wonderful gift." Sibella brushed Aleksander's arm and plucked something from him: a shining golden thread. It sank into her skin. Then she twisted her hands and raised a stack of logs. She laughed, but Aleksander, who'd been quiet, frowned.

"It must be some force," he said. "Something infecting us, that makes these things happen."

"Oh, stop fretting," said Sibella. "Enjoy it."

But Aleksander looked away. "What would my father think, Sibella? His son ... hex-addled. Who's ever heard of a hex-addled Lord?" He studied his hands.

Sibella's expression clouded with worry. She reached down, picked two white flowers – just like the one Erskin had touched – and offered one to Aleksander. "A flower of remembering," Sibella said. "They collect the memories of the person who picks them, and those memories keep them alive long after they've been pulled from the ground." When he didn't take it from her, she tucked the flower behind Aleksander's golden pin which bore his family crest.

"There," she said. "So, you can hold it and know that I believe in you, even if your father doesn't."

Aleksander reached up to the pin, frowning. His face was close to Erskin's. She reached out but touched nothing – instead the vision swirled and faded.

Erskin spun round. Now the couple were walking in a cave, weaving between glittering stalactites and stalagmites. Suddenly the Lordsson stopped, his attention caught by something flapping and flailing on the wall – a crag bat had somehow got itself tangled in a strong, razor-like web. Aleksander pulled it free and it lay dazed in his hands, its beautiful brown, furry belly rising and falling. The strange fibres of the web had injured the bat, and golden strands of luma, just like those Erskin had seen before now, tangled over the wound.

"What's this?" Aleksander said, prodding at the luma, which stuck to him and pulled away from the creature's body. The bat screeched as pain brought it round, and fluttered away fast on its two sets of wings, out of the Lordsson's grasp.

"Fascinating!" said Sibella, peering over his shoulder.

Aleksander was still staring at the luma strands when his attention was drawn to the cave wall. Behind where the bat had been was a golden crystal, with more of the glittering luma threads hanging around it. Its glow made the Lordsson's eyes gleam, and not in a nice way. "Can you feel its power?" he said to Sibella. "This has to be what's giving us our magic. Mountainfell must be full of it. It's just … natural. It grows in the soil, in the rock. Don't you see, Sibella? If my father knew, we wouldn't have to live in fear of this place any longer."

"No, Aleksander," Sibella said, reaching for his hands. "Don't tell him. If he knows the magic is something tangible" – she touched the golden strings – "he might want it for himself."

But Aleksander no longer seemed to be listening. Instead, he muttered, as if to himself, "My father will be so proud of me when he sees what I've learned. We don't need to be afraid of the mountain any more. Maybe we can even use this to help the village."

Darkness closed in around Erskin. All she could now hear was the sound of her own rapid breathing. Then a voice – Aleksander's.

"Sibella. I told my father about what we found." There was a flash of lightning and for an instant Erskin saw Aleksander's face, lit in blue, before being plunged into inky blackness again. He was in the cabin that he'd built with Sibella, rain now clattering against the windows.

"Aleksander. How could you?" came Sibella's voice. "We can't trust him with it. He'll only try to use it, and we have no idea how that will affect the mountain."

"That's just it, my love," came Aleksander's voice again, as thunder rolled. "He already knew! He has done for years. There's a machine – something developed on the mainland, for extracting it. My father's had one built here, deep underground where no one will find it. A drell. It's turning the luma into something that can be sold. It's desirable on the mainland, worth a fortune, and we have so much of it! That's why he kept the villagers in fear of the mountain, to keep them away from the truth. He isn't angry about my magic. He's glad! He thinks we can use it to make the drell even more powerful."

Another flash of lightning, dim this time – followed by thunder.

"I'm going to help him," the Lordsson continued. "Finally, I can make use of this ... magic of mine, to build the drell even bigger, even *stronger*. This is something only I can do, and it's my one chance to prove myself to Father... I'm sorry, Sibella. As the future Lord of Lofotby, I can't let him down."

The whole world seemed to turn upside down, and Erskin was in mist. It was raining, but the rain went right through her, as if she wasn't really there. The cabin was gone, but Sibella was there, drenched, and so was Aleksander. And someone else was with them, standing behind Aleksander. His father, the Lord.

"I won't let you do this," Sibella cried above the sound of the rain. "I'll tell everyone what you're doing here, and all the harm it's causing."

Aleksander was about to say something, but his father interrupted. "No one would believe you, witch," he said with a snarl. "Not when we tell the village that all the rumours about you are true and that's exactly what you are. Get away from here. Don't speak to my son again."

"Aleksander?" Sibella stared at Aleksander, who shifted uncomfortably, reaching a hand to touch the golden pin with its two, joined spirals. Then his face darkened. "My father's right," he said, though he couldn't look at her. "This is my duty, to my family." He sucked in a deep breath. Was that rain running down his face, or tears? "As future Lord of Lofotby, I hereby banish you from the village. Don't let us see you again," he added, "or—"

The rain intensified. Sibella staggered back as though she'd been stung. Then the Lordsson screamed. He and his father turned and fled. Erskin looked just in time to see Torkel, snaking out from the mist, from the low clouds, towards Sibella – as if to grab her...

The vision faded as quickly as it had begun. Erskin was on the floor in Sibella's home – the flower beside her. She picked herself up and didn't go near the flower again. The whole experience had left her shaken – but now, at least, she understood how Sibella knew that Aleksander and his father were behind the drell.

Outside the dragon roared and circled down, coming closer and closer, until a great thud shook the timbers, and the dragon landed in a giant coil around Sibella's house. Scrat zipped under the sofa in a flash.

Erskin backed away from the flower and ran to join her friends. She vowed that she would tell Leif what she'd seen stored in the flower as soon as they were in the air. He deserved to know.

The moons were already bright overhead as Erskin joined Leif outside, although eventide wasn't upon them yet. They had a good few hours until the sun would fully set, and hopefully by then they would be underground. Erskin wasn't looking forward to going near the drell, but she didn't fancy being in the Enchanted Forest after dark either.

Torkel looked just as magnificent up close as Erskin remembered, but in this light the wisps of the dragon's mane shone like threads of silk, and their scales glittered like stars. She turned to them, "Good to see you again, friend," said Erskin, resting her hand in Torkel's mane.

You too, little one.

Sibella helped them heave giant backpacks over their shoulders. "Take care of yourselves," she said.

Erskin and Leif glanced at each other, confused. "You mean you aren't coming?" Erskin said.

Sibella shook her head. "No. I can't go near the drell. And besides, I mustn't be seen. Aleksander likely thinks I'm dead, and it's better that way. But I'll be watching." She took Erskin's hand and rubbed her finger over the little raised sting. It looked less angry now and didn't hurt or itch – and Sibella's touch made it feel cool and soothed. "I will help however I can."

Erskin smiled. "Thank you, Sibella. We'll try our best to shut off the drell and put a stop to these tremors. I promise."

But when Erskin turned to leave, Sibella kept hold of her hand. "Wait. About your sister."

Instant anxiety wriggled in Erskin's stomach. The witch looked serious. "If it turns out that she was too badly injured. If she's ... if it's bad news." Sibella held Erskin's gaze and her hand, and Leif moved in close beside her.

"Go on."

"There is a place in the Enchanted Forest where spirits can, for a time, linger. Those who die, on the mountain."

An iciness crawled through Erskin's body at the word "die". She didn't want to think that that might have happened to Birgit. She couldn't. She just wanted for them all to keep searching, to keep believing that she was OK while she and Leif found the drell. Erskin shook her head. "But Torkel saw her. She's still alive."

"She was then," said Sibella, holding Erskin's hand tight so that she couldn't wriggle away. "But things can change quickly on the mountain. Especially for those who aren't used to the terrain. Especially if you're injured. I can talk to the creatures, thanks to the luma I took from Torkel. But they are still wild, as I've told you. I can only control a handful at any one time, and even that needs focus. Ultimately, they will follow their natures..."

Erskin scowled and looked away, not wanting to think about what that could mean.

"Listen, child. If the worst *has* happened and Birgit's spirit is at the waterfall in the forest, at least you'll know. You'll be able to say your goodbyes." Finally, Sibella let Erskin's hand fall.

Erskin felt utterly numb. It was too much to think about right now. Her mind was still reeling when she felt Leif rest his hand on her shoulder, and gently squeeze.

"Come on, Erskin. We should get going," he said softly. "The more progress we can make before dark, the better."

The pair of them took their leave of the witch and turned. Erskin took one step and nearly fell over a lump on the ground in front of her.

"Mooww."

"Scrat." Erskin bent down to fuss and kiss him, but when he tried to jump up around her neck, she stopped him. "No, Scrat. It's better if you stay here where it's safe," she said, though the thought of leaving him tugged at her heart. "I can't risk you getting hurt again. Anyway, we'll have to go underground *and* ride on Torkel's back, and you'll hate that."

"MOOWWW!" Scrat's tail shot out straight with the effort of his shout, and he stared her right in the eye.

Erskin actually drew back in shock. She'd never seen such defiance before in her life.

From behind them, Sibella laughed. "I don't think that's your decision to make," she called. "Fluffkins has clearly made up his own mind."

Together, the children clambered up onto Torkel's back and clung on tight – Scrat tucked up inside Erskin's jumper for safety. Just as before, the dragon rocked from side to side, and then they were rocketing up into the sky. Flying – and screaming.

25

IT WAS ALL JUST AS INCREDIBLE AS BEFORE. IN seconds they could see the vast expanse of the mountainside that wouldn't have been visible from the ground – not all at once, like they were seeing it now. The lush ancient forest where they were heading. The village lights twinkling far, far below. And in between... Erskin's mouth dropped open. Behind her, she heard Leif gasp. "Oh, Life, it's horrible."

Torkel twisted against the wind to give them a better view, and Erskin could see that glint of something tearing through the ground – the thing she and Leif had seen from the trees. Only from this height, she could make out what it really was: metal. Great ugly pipes dug under the mountain's skin like the many spines of a sea creature. It was definitely

some sort of machine. There was no doubt about it –
it must have been made by human hands.

From up here, it was clear that it was damaging
the mountain too. Out from the machine site spread
pale, barren, drained earth, just like the type they'd
crossed, part of which she'd seen from the marsh
tree – and a network of cracks spreading out from it
like a spider's web.

Erskin felt sick.

Now you see it, thought Torkel. *The Beast of the
Mountain, that the humans brought here. It eats,
and eats.*

A flash of the dragon's grief rolled through Erskin
in a sudden wave, and an image of the egg, alone,
being drained of its luma, its light, flared in her mind.
An understanding settled on Erskin as if it had always
been there: the egg needed to absorb luma to grow.
Without it... The dragon was thinking of their baby,
and their anguish became Erskin's.

"We aren't like the people who did this, Torkel,"
said Erskin, blinking back tears.

A low rumble came from the dragon's belly –
almost a purr, or the way someone might shush a baby
to soothe them. *I know that now, little one,* they said.
*The village's leader brought the beast here when it
was weak and small. The Leader's child – the Hollow*

One – helped it to grow bigger and stronger than the mountain can bear.

Erskin guessed that by "the village's leader", Torkel meant the Lord of Lofotby, meaning the Hollow One was Aleksander.

Together, the Hollow One and his Ampa created the Beast of the Mountain as it is now, Torkel continued. Erskin puzzled for a moment over what sounded to her like "Ampa" – the nearest her mind could relate it to was "parent".

Sibella knew the truth, Torkel went on, *but the Leader and the Hollow One told lies to the villagers, casting her as dangerous and evil, so that she wouldn't be believed. She was banished from the village, so she fled here – to Mountainfell. And this is where I came across her. The future Witch of the Mountain.* Torkel let out a gentle grunt, remembering. *She was afraid of me then. She thought I was going to eat her.* A strange rumble came from Torkel's throat, like a small chuckle.

Erskin told Leif everything. For a while they flew in silence.

All this time, Erskin had believed the stories she'd heard, about the Lordsson's sweetheart being hex-addled, and turning her back on the village. And how the Lordsson had only wanted to protect Lofotby from the dangerous mountain. But now, so many of those stories were being turned upside down. He and his father had banished Sibella here.

Erskin had to turn away from the drell's damage – she couldn't bear to look at it any more. As she looked up, Erskin glimpsed the mainland on the other side of Mountainfell. A whole mountain range – though none as grand as their own – levelled out into smaller hills, and the vast cities, with plains and woods and craters and walls... Erskin had never seen any of this before. She never dreamed she could. Nor that it would be possible to ride a dragon.

They drew nearer and nearer to the ancient forest, until Torkel was bringing them down close to its edge. *This is as far as I can take you. Be safe on your journey, my little ones.*

"Thank you, Torkel," said Erskin, and told Leif everything the dragon had said.

Leif rested his hand on Torkel's mane, and together they all wished each other well before the dragon took off again.

A roar echoed out as Torkel snaked above them, scales glowing like ghostly mist.

You must stop the humans' beast, and please, look for my egg, my Torkelchild, came their final words in Erskin's mind. *You must hurry. The witch and I will not stop searching for your sister.*

"We will, Torkel," Erskin replied. She found that if she spoke the words, she projected them with her mind naturally. "We'll try as hard as we can. And we'll try our hardest to find the egg too."

In response, Torkel said something with their feelings that Erskin's brain couldn't quite translate. It was a farewell, she knew that much. And it filled her with a sense of peace. But the closest she could get to it in words was, *Life is precious*.

It was much colder up here, and frost had turned everything silver. It looked dazzling against an almost violet eventide sky, and Erskin was glad of her living, breathing scarf of pure fluff – even if it did shout at her occasionally. Having Scrat with her made Erskin feel whole again. And with Leif by her side too she felt stronger than ever.

The sky above them morphed to a crisp, mid-blue as they made their way into the first sparse smattering of trees at the edge of the Enchanted Forest. Icicles hung from the rocks and branches, and the sound of drips and trickles became the mountain's own music as melted ice formed little rivulets. The smell of green lushness that had been missing on the lower slopes filled their lungs. They stopped to collect more water from a small stream. The trek became steeper as they climbed. Erskin found that catching her breath became more of a chore.

"This place really doesn't seem as bad as all that to me," said Leif as they went. "Not the way Sibella was talking anyway."

Erskin wasn't so sure. She hoped they wouldn't run into any more of the big cats without Sibella or the dragon here to help them. Lissenynx, Leif had called them. He'd been studying Sibella's books, and had even brought *The Mountain Creature Compendium* and *Mountain Botany* with them for the journey.

According to the books, lissenynx had the quietest tread and most sensitive hearing of any creature, thanks to their big ears and luma – and they could hear the rustle of a cob mouse several miles away. Erskin thought of her sister, lost and hurt. What if a wild lissenynx snuck up on her?

As they trudged, the forest grew denser, the trees crowded more tightly together. The children stayed alert for anything that moved and kept a count of the creatures they saw, looking them up in Sibella's books as they went. Four shadow hares. Six tellerhawks, circling in the air. Two rainbow-wing moths dancing with each other over the grass, leaving a colour trail. And one tiny cob mouse, which zipped away in a cloud of dust as soon as it saw them, using its super speed.

Leif told her that the creatures on the lower slopes had been wood foxes, and the bird Erskin had healed was a burrowbird, which hibernated in the warmth of tree roots and sometimes – though this was merely a folk legend – granted wishes.

Erskin thought of the wishes she'd made: for Scrat to be alive and Birgit to be safe from the dragon. She could kick herself for not simply wishing that Birgit was alive too, and wondered again where her sister was now.

26

THEY'D WALKED FOR HOURS, AND ERSKIN AND LEIF were exhausted. Eventide drew in quickly, deepening the shadows, marking the first night Erskin would spend away from her sister; from home. She wondered how her parents were doing. They'd lost both their daughters – one to a dragon, the other to being headstrong and foolish. They must be worried sick.

Shafts of stubborn, buttery light gleamed through the trees and glinted off drifting donderline seeds. Erskin reached out and managed to catch one in the cage of her hand. She remembered the ones she'd seen in the square – only yesterday. Birgit had been beside her then.

She cupped the seed in her hand. Their mam had said that catching one could mean someone is missing you. Holding the seed made her feel calmer, and she was reminded suddenly of how Birgit would place a hand on her shoulder at night when she woke up and was afraid of the dark. Just her presence was enough to make Erskin feel safe and send her back to sleep. It was uncanny how Birgit had always seemed to know Erskin had woken before she'd even made a sound.

Erskin would have given anything to feel Birgit's reassuring hand on her shoulder right now. Her absence felt like a slow hollowing out of Erskin's insides: a terrible, dull ache. Erskin held the caught donderline seed against her cheek, thinking of Birgit, and then blew. Her breath made it swirl, until the breeze caught hold of it and carried it away among the trees. "I'm coming for you, Birgit," she whispered to the seed. "Don't be afraid." Watching it made Erskin's vision blur, and she staggered.

"Whoa," said Leif, catching her arm. "Are you OK?" He looked as exhausted as Erskin felt, but they had to keep going – for Birgit, for Torkel, and for Sibella.

Erskin nodded. "Just tired," she said.

Leif stopped abruptly and looked about him. "What did you say?"

Erskin frowned. "Just that I'm tired."

"Oh..." Leif shook his head. "I thought I heard

something... Um. I thought you said something else."
He looked through the trees.

From a great distance now, Torkel roared – they felt it more as a vibration through their feet. Even though they were too far away, Erskin still reached out to try and touch the dragon's mind – to let Torkel know she was there.

A paw reached down from Erskin's shoulder and tapped her gently on the arm. *Fuss. Want fuss*, came Scrat's thoughts.

Erskin smiled and stroked his head – his favourite spot for a tickle – though it wasn't long before she'd drifted into troubled thoughts about Birgit again. Her sister was stressed all the time. But then their mam and dad were always so busy, and it often fell on Birgit to look after Erskin. Perhaps Erskin hadn't appreciated how hard that had been for her sister; at the time she'd thought Birgit just wanted to be bossy and mean. At school, too, Birgit was always nagging her to stop being weird, to try and fit in, and making her feel bad when she couldn't. What if, in Birgit's head at least, she'd been trying to look out for her? Trying to help her be accepted, and keep her safe?

Erskin was so wrapped up in her own thoughts and imaginings a lot of the time that she didn't always see other people's situations clearly, and she realized now that she hadn't seen Birgit's. That thought made her hollowed-out feeling even worse. When Erskin finally saw her sister again, she vowed to try to understand her more.

Erskin swooned with tiredness and had to lean against some smooth bark. She looked around. There was no path, only trees. Every direction looked exactly the same, and it was getting darker by the second. Panic rose in her throat like a ball bobbing up in water.

"How do we even know we're going the right way? I think we're lost." She stared at Leif, who looked stricken too and scratched his head.

"Which way?" he mumbled under his breath. "Which way...?"

The trees up ahead rustled and creaked, even though there wasn't even the slightest breeze. Erskin and Leif clung to each other in fear as, in front of their eyes, the trees shifted. Erskin suppressed a scream: they were going to close in, attack them... But instead, a space opened up ahead. It looked very much like a path.

Erskin stared at Leif, who stared back. "I ... I wasn't sure before," he said in a small, shocked voice, "but now I'm certain." He stepped back and looked around. "I can hear them. The trees." More rustling came from all around, and his eyes grew even wider. "They say we should go this way."

"Leif, it's your luma!" Erskin gasped. Her mind whirred back to when they had fallen from Torkel's back. Hadn't Leif cried out for help then? And by some miracle they'd landed safely. It had to have been the trees who'd heard him, and helped.

Nervously, Leif held out a hand. "Erm," he said. "Hi?"

There was a rustle, and one leaf-laden branch reached down to touch his fingers, as if to introduce itself. Leif gawped at Erskin. "Yep," he said, and a beam broke out across his face. "I think you might be right."

From then on, every time they got stuck or confused, the trees would rustle and bend to reveal the right path. The trees seemed to like Leif – a lot. "I think they've been talking to me for a while," Leif said. "I just didn't really know it before. Or, maybe I wasn't listening properly. But I think that's why I kept being drawn to them."

Erskin had never known a forest that was so keen to help. It made her shiver a little to think what this place might be like if the trees *didn't* like you.

This time it was Leif's turn to stagger and almost fall from exhaustion. Erskin only just caught him in time. There was still no sign of the mountain caves but it was no good – they were going to have to sleep.

"We have to rest," said Erskin, who was nearly asleep on her feet. She could tell Leif wanted to keep on going as much as she did, but eventually he nodded.

"Yes," he agreed in a pained voice. "We do."

At Leif's words, the trees curved their branches around a mossy nook and transformed before their eyes into a canopy that would shelter them. Scrat hopped down from Erskin's shoulders, sauntered over, and started padding the ground with his paws. With one eyebrow raised, Erskin said, "Looks like Scrat's already made up his mind."

"Well, if it's good enough for Scrat..." Leif smiled. "We'll be warm under our blankets from Sibella's house too."

Erskin could barely keep her eyes open as they settled down in the mossy shelter. Just as she was dropping off, a small voice probed her mind. It was close, she was sure of it. She grabbed Leif's arm. "Shh," she whispered. "Look."

A deer with a single horn coming from its forehead stared right back at Erskin from a distance, as still as if it were a statue. Its beautiful brown eyes were rimmed with long, delicate eyelashes, and its horn gleamed gold in the weakening shafts of light that had grown ghostly now. Erskin's skin tingled as the leaves on the trees rustled. It was the most beautiful sight she'd ever seen.

"The deer eat a type of lichen off the trees," whispered Leif, "which stops the lichen getting out of control and smothering the bark. They love the uni-horned deer for it and encourage them to nest near by, by making secret grottos for them like this one and hiding them from predators, like the lissenynx." He returned Erskin's questioning look by jerking his head upwards at the trees and adding, "They told me." In response, came more rustling.

As they watched, the deer dipped its head, clearly deciding they were no threat, and silently ambled away.

The beetles. The trees. The uni-horned deer. Everything was different, and everything affected something else in an unbroken circle, Erskin realized. And everything, no matter what it was, belonged.

"Um, Erskin," said Leif close to Erskin's ear. His voice made her jump. She hadn't realized how close to drifting off she'd been – and he sounded grave. "What's wrong?"

"According to Sibella's book, we should be close to the Spirits' Waterfall."

Erskin's heart sank. "Birgit isn't there."

"But—"

"She isn't there!"

Leif rubbed the back of his head, and Erskin felt instantly bad for snapping.

"Leif, I'm sorry. I didn't mean it."

Leaves fluttered and boughs creaked. Leif paused, listening. "The trees say not to be afraid ... that death feeds new life."

Erskin flinched. She couldn't bear to think that her sister was ... dead.

When Leif went on his tone was softer. "I think Birgit is fine. We'll find her. I know we will but ... the trees say that the Spirits' Waterfall is a beautiful, peaceful place, hidden away so that hardly anything living ever finds its way there. They protect it," said Leif, chewing his cheek. "It might be worth seeing ... even though we know Birgit isn't there, of course."

Erskin hugged her arms and grew thoughtful. She knew that Leif was trying to be kind, but she could not accept the thought that her sister wasn't alive. She didn't need to go to the waterfall to check.

Troubled thoughts – of Birgit, the drell and all that lay before them – plagued her as she finally fell asleep.

27

DARKNESS. FEAR. AND THE GRINDING OF MACHINERY.

Erskin had never been one of those people who knew when they were dreaming, so it was odd that she noticed it now. Yet, somehow, she knew that this wasn't real. Or at least, that it wasn't happening to *her*.

Her eyes grew accustomed to the darkness and, with a jolt, she realized she'd seen this place before – in the nightmare she'd had, before she'd woken in Sibella's cabin. She was in a large hall with a high, blue ceiling, although the ceiling was now cracked right in two.

Another pulse of fear rolled through her, along with a terrible, overwhelming pain. It came in waves, keeping time with the unrelenting sound of the machine. She was getting weaker – ever weaker.

She tried to cry out for help, but to her horror the sound that came out wasn't words; it wasn't even a human cry.

It hit her all at once. Was Torkel's egg showing her this vision? Was their baby making contact with her?

Torkelchild, Erskin thought. *Can you hear me?*

But another surge of fear ran through her – through the egg, that was filling her up with its own feelings – and then she could hear footsteps coming closer and closer. With every step, Erskin felt the terror rising, her own now inseparable from the egg's.

Then a figure emerged from the gloom. It was a man wearing fine clothes embroidered with glinting gold and a golden pin on his lapel. He pressed his face close to the egg and smiled with pride. "My prize," he said, as if to himself. "To think I was lucky enough to find you. And now you're mine." It was Aleksander the Lordsson.

28

ERSKIN WOKE, TERRIFIED AND BREATHLESS, TO FEEL a hand on her shoulder. Her first thought was that she was four again, safe at home with Birgit. Then, with a start, she remembered everything. She lifted her head and looked around.

It was still night. Scrat was curled up in the crook of her arm, his furry silver belly rising and falling in sleep. Beyond him, Leif snored soundly. She considered waking him to tell him what she'd seen, but thought better of it. He would need all his strength for tomorrow – they both would.

What she'd thought had been a hand against her back was in fact a small nobble of tree root, poking through the moss. A wasp buzzed close to her face, weaving this way and that – before flying off through the trees. The sting on her hand twinged.

Now Erskin was awake, she couldn't get comfortable again. Her body felt stiff – she could do with stretching her legs. She snuck out of the nook and wandered a little way. It felt like she was in a dream state, somewhere between waking and sleeping. It was hard to tell if this was real or imagined.

The trees creaked slowly and rhythmically, as though snoring, and the forest floor was lit with a blue glow from the light of the two moons that made it through their branches. But there was something else Erskin could hear now, in the relative silence. The rushing of water, as if from a stream, or—

A waterfall.

Despite her earlier confidence that Birgit was safe, Erskin followed the sound to a wall of trees, standing tall together, like guards. She wasn't sure if she wanted to be here, and part of her wanted to go straight back to Leif and Scrat. But what if the trees were showing her this because Birgit's spirit *was* here? What if she really had already died, here on the mountain? No matter how hard it was, she had to accept that it was a possibility. If Birgit was here, she had to know...

She took a deep breath, and drew herself up. "OK." Erskin reached forward with a shaking hand. Her heart pumped hard in her chest.

Slowly, with a groan, one of the trees rolled aside. Erskin wondered if Leif had asked the trees to show her this place.

Beyond was what could only have been the Spirits' Waterfall. It was as beautiful as she'd imagined when Leif had described it. A majestic, gushing cascade feeding a sparkling, clear pool, with tiny streams leading off in all directions, and soft, moss-covered banks of the most vivid green Erskin had ever seen.

But it was totally empty. Erskin sobbed with relief.

Birgit wasn't there.

29

ERSKIN AND LEIF WOKE SNUG AND WARM INSIDE THE
enchanted nook that the forest had made for them.
Erskin rubbed her face. She couldn't remember how
she'd got back here, but she was certain she hadn't
dreamed the waterfall – plus her feet were caked with
dirt. In a sudden rush, she remembered her dream
about the egg: her vision. She told everything to
Leif, who listened with concern. "It sounds like the
Lordsson really does have the egg, and that it's close
to the drell. But why do you think it's made contact
with you, Erskin? Why not Torkel?"

Erskin shook her head. "I don't think Torkel can
hear it. I think the drell hurts them too much, since
luma is in their bones. I'm not sure whether the egg
even knows what it's doing – it's just reaching out …
to anyone. I can hear it because the drell doesn't affect

me in the same way." Either way, Erskin knew the egg didn't have long. It was getting weaker by the moment as the drell drained its luma, and with it its life force.

They ate a hasty breakfast and packed away their blankets. Outside their nook, a thin mist hung in layers around the tree trunks. Besides which, everything looked different to the night before. "Have the trees moved around?" asked Erskin, frowning. Her heart began to tap a faster rhythm.

Last night she'd gone to sleep feeling safe on the mountain for the first time, believing the trees were looking after them and wouldn't plot to get them lost, as the stories had told. But now she felt on edge. The forest had definitely changed, and so had its mood.

Leif scratched his head and studied the map. "I'm not sure."

Their onward journey went from bad to worse.

"I think we're walking in circles," Erskin said after a while. "I'm sure we've been this way before. What's going on, Leif?"

"I don't know!" Leif ran his hands through his hair. "I just don't understand it. They keep telling me this is the right way, but…"

This was bad. The trees had been so helpful yesterday, but now something had changed. Were they actually *trying* to confuse them? Is this what had really happened to the Lordsson's "offerings" to the dragon – those who even got this far?

From somewhere among the trees came a distinctive snarl.

The children stared at each other, and Leif gulped. Around Erskin's neck, Scrat's hackles rose, and he hissed.

"Come on." Erskin grabbed Leif's sleeve and pulled. Together they plunged deeper into the forest, but they only seemed to lose their sense of direction even more. The trees closed in and it became darker; the sounds of the forest more threatening. From somewhere up ahead came what sounded like a scream. Erskin's blood ran cold.

Before she could stop him, Scrat leaped from her shoulders. *Scrat go look!* He turned his wild face at them and screeched, before disappearing into the mists of a thicket.

"Scrat, wait!" Erskin cried, but he was already gone.

Panic gripped Erskin and she sprinted after him with Leif close on her heels, crashing into trees and tripping on brambles. "Stop, Erskin!"

But Erskin didn't want to lose Scrat again – especially not here. "Scrattletak, where are you?" she called. Then, in her mind: *SCRAT. Come back.*

The mist got thicker. Erskin could hardly see a thing. She put one hand out in front of her and held on to Leif's with the other so they wouldn't get separated. Her heart pounded. Where was that daft cat?

Leif pulled her back. "Erskin, we can't get distracted now. We have to find our way out of here."

"But what about Scrat..." Panic filled Erskin to bursting. She breathed faster and faster but still couldn't get enough air.

Leif held her firm. "Scrat can take care of himself," he said. "He found his way back to Sibella's once already – remember?"

With tears in her eyes, Erskin nodded. That was true. She had to trust that Scrat could find his own way. But the children barely had time to take another step when they heard another scream, followed by a snarl – much louder this time. The trees around them rustled. A sharp pain sliced through Erskin's skull – and at the same time a voice, clear and loud, spoke inside it.

Run.

Leif stopped and groaned. He must have been overwhelmed by the sharp pain too. The voice. Had Leif heard it? There was no time to wonder. They both clutched at their ears as the voice spoke again, louder this time.

Run!

Adrenalin flooded Erskin's legs and it was all she could do to hold still. The urge to obey the voice – to run the other way – was overwhelming. But before she could turn and flee, something caught Erskin's eye through the trees up ahead.

"What's that?" It looked like something was moving there. A figure emerged from the mist. It was sprinting towards them, gaining ground every second. The voice resounded in her head again, but this time the figure spoke aloud too.

"RUN!"

RUN!

Erskin gasped.

It was Birgit.

30

"DIDN'T YOU HEAR ME?" BIRGIT SHRIEKED. "I SAID RUN!"

She was about to plough straight into them. Even if either of them could have resisted the urge to run any longer, they didn't have a choice. They turned and fled.

And they were just in time.

A fierce snarl came from behind them. Erskin glanced behind her and saw a dark shape tearing through the trees and mist towards them, all teeth and claws. Erskin screamed. It growled again, closer this time – whatever had been chasing Birgit was now after them, too. "Trees, please help us!" cried Leif in desperation. Erskin called out in her mind to Torkel, to Sibella – but who knew if either would hear her?

All at once, the trees around them rustled, and suddenly branches were reaching down for them. Leif made a jump for it, grabbed a branch and swung himself up. Erskin made the jump too, but her fingers slipped and she fell back down.

Right then Birgit barrelled into her. She scooped Erskin up into the branches and then hoisted herself up too, with Leif's help.

A small, fierce beast snapped at their heels, missing by a hair's breadth, as the tree branches raised them higher, lifting them out of harm's way. Birgit landed on top of Erskin as they were flung forward and one arm wrapped around her younger sister's body, the long dark curtain of Birgit's hair falling over Erskin's face.

The creature was pacing around the trunk of the tree, snapping and snarling in a frenzy – but there came a buzzing sound and a small insect flew at the creature's face, followed by another. Sibella's wasps, they had to be. And, just as quickly as the ferocious beast had appeared, it fled back into the mist.

All fell silent. "Wolvereyes," panted Leif. Sweat had plastered his hair to his forehead. "Fiercest when they smell blood." ·

Erskin looked up at her sister, barely able to believe it was her. Birgit had dried blood on her forehead, and some on her clothes.

Birgit stared back, fraught with worry. "Erskin," she said in a shaking voice.

"Birgit!" Erskin flung her arms around Birgit's neck and dragged her down into a hug. Before she even knew it, she was sobbing into Birgit's dark hair: their mother's hair.

"I thought I'd lost you," Erskin said to Birgit in a cracked voice. "I'm sorry, I'm so sorry for everything."

"Me too," said Birgit. They hugged for a long time. But when Birgit moved back, she was grinning. "I knew you had to be close," she said, "because of that ridiculous cat of yours." She nodded to the ground where Scrat was rubbing against the base of the tree.

"Prrow." *Scrat find present – other human! Nice present. You like, I know.* He began to lick his paw.

"Scrattletak!" Erskin clambered down and took him in her arms. "Don't run off like that again, you big fluffball. Please." Scrat purred; he enjoyed being stroked. Erskin turned her attention back to Birgit, who climbed down next to her. She was so relieved to see her sister that she couldn't help beaming.

"Hey. What's this on your face?" Erskin peeled something off Birgit's cheek with her nails. It was a flattened donderline seed. *"Catch a donderline seed..."* Erskin began.

"… *It could mean someone is missing you, too,*" Birgit finished. "You know this could even be the one I was following." She glanced at Erskin. "I'd been stuck in this forest for hours and then it appeared, and I don't know why, but I just followed it. It reminded me of Mam's stories, and of home. And … you. And then I found Scrat." She paused. "Did you…?"

Erskin nodded and hugged her again. Mountainfell truly was a magical place.

"What on Yor are you two doing here, anyway?" asked Birgit. "Where are the rest of the rescue party?" She looked about.

"There's … just us," Erskin said in a quiet voice.

"You came up here, *alone*?" Birgit's eyes widened. "For me? Erskin, you could've been killed. What were you—" But she stopped herself, and said instead, "I'm just glad you're not hurt. And … relieved that you found me."

"I came too, so she wasn't totally alone," said Leif shyly, as the tree lowered him to the ground. "Although it was a little bit by accident, to be fair."

Birgit gave the pair a puzzled look. Erskin couldn't help but laugh.

A wave of exhaustion seemed to roll over Birgit then and Erskin remembered the dried blood caked onto her sister's skin. "Birgit, you're bleeding…"

"No, not any more. I'm all right." Her sister rubbed her arms. "That's from when the dragon dropped me. I was lucky the tree branches broke my fall, or I wouldn't be here. Anyway, I've been managing to stay a step ahead of everything that's been trying to eat me. I've been getting this strange – feeling." Birgit glanced between Erskin and Leif, and grew even more pale beneath the dirt and blood. "It's always right before I run into danger. It's like I can sense something bad coming, and my head sends out a kind of signal – like a warning pulse. What's happening to me, Erskin?" she added in a small voice.

Erskin gasped. "It's your luma." Of course. It had to be. Erskin had never considered the fact that Birgit might have her own magic.

Birgit frowned and looked more worried than ever. "What's luma?"

Erskin stared at Leif, and then back to Birgit. "This – 'warning pulse'. Did you know it reached us?" she asked. "It told us to run."

"Did it? I just had this feeling that something really, really bad was going to happen, right before that … creature appeared. The 'thought' thing just happened."

"It's your magic, and it saved our lives. Well – yours warned us about the wolvereye and then Leif's helped us into this tree together. Also, I think Sibella sent her wasps to protect us..." Erskin trailed off. Birgit's eyes had begun to fill with tears.

"*Magic?*" Birgit hugged her arms. "You mean— I'm" – she spoke in a whisper – "hex-addled?"

"Yes," Erskin said. She put her arms around her sister, holding her tight. "But it's not what you think it is. It's OK. You don't have to be afraid any more. I'll tell you everything."

31

THE CHILDREN – THREE OF THEM NOW, AND SCRAT – still had to find their way out of the Enchanted Forest. They carried on, growing more and more desperate. Erskin spun around, her heart pounding, searching for the right direction. So did Leif. But when Erskin turned back, she stopped dead. The way ahead was blocked by a tightly packed wall of trees – an impenetrable thicket – that hadn't been there a moment ago.

"Ah," said Leif, finally. "I think I know what's going on here." To Erskin's surprise, he didn't sound as frightened as she was. He took a deep breath and lowered his voice. "The trees don't want us to leave."

Erskin shivered. "What? Why not?"

"I think they're frightened," he said. He frowned as though straining to listen. "The drell scares them and they don't want us to go near it and get hurt. These trees are closer to the drell, so they're more afraid of it. Basically, they like us, and want to keep us safe."

"That's all very well," said Birgit, folding her arms. "But I don't want to be stuck here for the rest of my life." Her voice was shaky, and Erskin guessed she was still reeling from everything they'd told her about Mountainfell – and luma. She hadn't been happy when she'd heard about their plan to destroy the drell – not at all. But she'd reluctantly agreed to go along with it.

Leif held up his hand. "Hang on. Let me speak to them." He turned around to face the thicket and cleared his throat. "Excuse me," he said. "Hello there, trees. It's been nice to meet you and everything. But we really need to get going..." The leaves above and around them trembled. "Come on now," said Leif, as if in reply. "I know you're scared but, please, show us the way. We're here to make the drelling stop."

The trees rustled again.

"Oh, we've loved being here too," said Leif, his tone brightening. "And it's not that we don't *want* to stay. It's just that— Yes, we had a great night's sleep, thank you. Very comfy. No, no, not at all, it was very warm."

Erskin rolled her eyes. She couldn't believe this

was happening. Would the trees try keeping them here with chit-chat now too? "Tell them that unless they let us go, the loss of luma will just get worse," she suggested. "The whole mountain could be affected unless the drelling stops. And that's what we're going to do – stop it."

"Moowww," agreed Scrat.

The trees must have heard Erskin, because they shook as if a heavy gust of wind had blown through them, and the sound of rustling spread out behind them for what seemed like miles, until the whole forest might well have been joining in.

Leif paused, listening. Then he whispered, "They're talking it over now."

"Talking what over?" Erskin whispered back with urgency. "Whether or not they'll let us go? They wouldn't keep us here *for ever*, would they?"

Birgit's eyes widened and a nearby noise made her jump. She stepped closer to her sister. Leif only shrugged.

The rustling stopped and the trees fell deathly silent. Erskin, Leif and Birgit waited. Finally, there came a slow, creaking sound. The thicket stayed where it was, but the ground shifted beneath it. Soil turned over and roots wormed out like fingers, raking back the earth. Erskin stepped back, remembering in a flash the chasm and Scrat's fall. Her head spun and her pulse began thumping.

A root-lined hole in the ground opened up. Erskin realized with a start what it was. The trees had made a shortcut into the mountain tunnels so the children wouldn't need to travel to the cave mouths, far above. Yet despite her gratitude, Erskin gulped. It would be barely big enough for them to squeeze through, so they'd need to leave their bags behind. And it was pitch black in there.

"Thank you all," said Leif, hugging the nearest tree. "I swear we'll do our best to stop the drell from taking luma. And we'll definitely come to visit you again. Very soon. No, we won't leave it too long. I promise."

Erskin took one last glance behind her. She was searching for Torkel's mind, to say goodbye – and to get a final glimpse of the sky for what might be a long time. But what she saw turned her whole body to stone. Leif looked to see what Erskin was staring at, and gasped.

The trees behind them had shifted to give a clear view across the sweep of lower mountain. They could see just how high they'd climbed, but also a deep, wide crack that spanned a huge distance across the mid and lower slopes. It snaked and spread out like a dark root through the earth, reaching spidery fingertips towards the village far below. Erskin was sure it hadn't been there yesterday when they'd ridden Torkel. She'd seen the drell site then: the spreading, cracking ring of dry land, and the circle of the Creeping Marsh, but she definitely hadn't seen this.

"That must have been getting worse with the tremors since yesterday," she mumbled to Leif, who nodded, still staring at it with horror. It looked unstable. If any of that damaged section were to come away from the mountain, the village could be crushed. There was no time to lose; they had to stop the drell.

Birgit cried, "What on Yor *is* that? Ugh, it's horrible!" She clutched at her stomach, as if she'd felt something just by looking at it. As she did so, a warning pulse from Birgit came into Erskin's head, wordless this time, and more faint, but still a warning – of danger.

It was time to head into the hole. First, Erskin turned to her sister. "Are you OK about all this, Birgit?" She was worried about her. Birgit had been through so much, and although they'd given her their supplies to eat and drink, she still looked exhausted.

Birgit folded her arms. "I don't have much choice, do I?" she said, rolling her eyes. "I'm not staying here. Anyway" – her voice took on a softer edge – "if you say you need to do this then I'm with you." The shadow of a weak smile crossed Birgit's lips, and Erskin smiled too. "I'm going through first, though," Birgit said, pushing past, and without another word disappeared into the hole.

Next, Erskin put Scrat down in front of it. *Go on, Scrattletak. It's OK. I'll be right behind you.* This is why she'd wanted to leave him with Sibella. She wasn't sure how Scrat would take being underground. But then, he'd found his way out of the tunnels before – so perhaps this wouldn't be new to him, after all.

Scrat gave a mew, swished his tail and slunk in. Erskin took a deep breath, crouched down and crawled in after him. If it wasn't for hearing Leif behind her, exchanging polite courtesies with the trees and making more promises to pay a return visit, she might not have had the courage to keep going all the way into the mouth of the hole and the darkness within.

32

THE HOLE SEEMED TO GET NARROWER THE FURTHER Erskin went. Her heart pounded in her ears and her mind screamed at her to turn back. It felt unnatural to climb into a tight space like this *on purpose*. Yet every time she faltered or got a little stuck, a tree root gave her a nudge.

Finally, the hole opened out into a wider space, a faint golden glow coming from somewhere. In spite of her faded strength, Birgit helped Erskin through as she glanced all around with wary eyes. This had to be one of the access tunnels to the drell that Sibella had described.

They could see again and also stand – that's all Erskin cared about. As soon as Leif had clambered through, the hole that the trees had held open for them creaked, shrank, and closed to nothing. Erskin wiped the cold sweat from her forehead, but it was Leif who spoke first.

"Phew," he said under his breath. "I love trees, but all that small talk wore me out. I hope they're not all like that. I'll never get any peace."

"Maybe it's just the ancient ones." Erskin stifled a nervous chuckle. "I suppose they don't meet many humans who can talk to them like you can."

The tunnel took them in a downward spiral immediately, in twists and turns like a labyrinth. The air was stifling. Sweat broke out across Erskin's top lip and all around her hairline as they got further inside – further away from fresh air and sky.

"How do we know … we're going the right way?" asked Leif, in gasps. "The trees thought this tunnel would connect with the drell further down. I hope they're right. I don't want to keep walking for ever." He seemed to dislike the enclosed space, the darkness, as much as Erskin did.

Birgit wasn't coping well either; Erskin could tell by how fast she was breathing. She grabbed her elder sister's hand. "Try not to panic," she told her. "Take deep breaths."

Birgit nodded. "I can't tell what's dangerous and what isn't in here," she said through gasps. "It *all* feels wrong."

Something was up with Scrat, too, who sniffed everything and kept stopping to roll in the dirt and wail. But then Scrat sat up, his ears shooting upright. "Mow."

Erskin stopped and listened. Sure enough, there came the rhythmic hum she'd heard in her nightmares, somewhere deeper in. The regular, working sounds of a machine. They had to be getting closer to whatever mechanism powered the drell.

Leif and Erskin stared at each other. All they had to do was follow the sound.

After a while Erskin lost all sense of time. It felt like they'd been walking for hours, but it could have been minutes – who could say?

The machine's hum grew louder. The cave walls sparkled and gave off a luminous golden glow that reminded Erskin of candlelight that didn't flicker. She ran her finger across the surface. It was some kind of crusty sediment. Only further on, where the sediment formed large crystals, did she realize what it actually was. Luma. She stared at it in awe as Leif and Birgit joined her.

Birgit gasped. Erskin had seen luma like this before, she realized. In the vision she'd had of Sibella and Aleksander. It was strange to think how much she'd feared "hex magic". Now she didn't feel scared – just curious. She could actually feel a tension around her like you get before lightning – as if the air was charged.

Strands of gold were drifting out of the crystals and floating away down the tunnel – pulled by some invisible force. All three children watched them go. And, as the strands were tugged away, the glow of the crystals began to dim.

Birgit cried out. "Look!" When she held up her hand, Erskin and Leif saw that tiny, golden wisps were coming out of it to follow the rest. It was happening to the others too.

Erskin tried to project some words to Scrat, but he just mewled and tried to catch the disappearing luma in his claws. "Our abilities," Erskin said to Leif and Birgit. "I think they're being weakened. Like Sibella said."

The drell. It had to be. Erskin clenched her jaw, but at least this meant they were going in the right direction.

"Look," hissed Leif. "What's this?" He ran further down the tunnel to study a wire of some sort embedded in the rock. The more they looked the more they found. Not just wires, but long, metal cylinders cutting into the rock too. Tiny hairline cracks spidered out from the metal, and when Erskin scratched at it, small shards of the rock flaked away. The luma strands were gathering around it and getting sucked inside.

The machinery led in the same direction down the tunnel. It looked shiny and new.

"This must all be part of the drell," said Erskin. She ran her hand over yet more of the shiny silver and copper-coloured wires that dug, needle-like, into the mountain's skin. Her stomach twisted. "I had no idea the drell stretched this far underground," she mumbled. They must have seen only a fraction of it from the sky, on the surface.

"Erskin," said Leif, his eyes twinkling. "What if we tried to break these wires?"

They stared at each other. Then Erskin clawed at the wires, trying to get enough purchase to pull them out. Leif did the same. She managed to rip two of the smallest out of the wall and left them dangling. Together she and Leif started tugging at one of the bigger metal tentacles.

"Stop, Erskin!" It was Birgit. "Don't be an idiot. You'll hurt yourself." When Erskin stared, Birgit instantly looked sheepish. "I'm sorry," she said. "I didn't mean to call you an idiot. But there must be a better way to do it. That'll take for ever. Here." She scrambled around on the floor, then handed Erskin and Leif a big rock each. She picked up one of her own and smashed the metal with it three times.

The rock made a dent the first two times, and then a gash. Glittering golden threads of luma began to leak out and pool at Birgit's feet.

Erskin and Leif stared with their mouths open. This was a side of Birgit that Erskin had never seen: her sister, who did as she was told and never put a foot wrong. But she'd been right, it definitely was more effective. The children began breaking the metal wires as quickly as they could. But this was only a fraction of the drell. They needed to destroy a much more essential part of the machinery if they were going to stop it properly.

They ran further down the tunnel. The machine-like hum grew louder and louder, until the passage opened out, and they found themselves in a cavern filled with metal tubes. This had to be the heart of the drell, the place where all the wires led. For a moment they stood in stunned silence – before getting to work with their rocks. The drell's humming became a terrible grinding, scraping sound, and slowed.

Strange noises echoed down the tunnel. It sounded like … voices. Erskin, Leif and Birgit froze.

"Did you…?"

"Hear that too...?"

"MOOWWW. Moouueewww." Scrat started making weird sounds as the noises coming from the depths of the tunnel grew louder. Now they could see the flash of glow lamps. Goosebumps rose on Erskin's arms. It sounded like human voices. And they were coming this way.

"Quick," shrilled Birgit. "Hide!" But it was too late. There was barely time for Scrat to clamber up around Erskin's neck before the tunnel ahead was filled with people. They all wore the same overalls, each with a symbol on them: the double spiral from the cairn – the Lordsson's family crest.

"What are you doing here?" asked the man in front.

Erskin blinked. There was something strangely familiar about him, but she couldn't figure out what.

"Alrick?" Leif cried out.

And then Erskin realized. It was Alrick Olsen – one of "the missing", whose name was now carved on the remembrance wall.

33

Erskin stared.

Confusion clouded Alrick's face, but when he saw Leif, his eyes widened. "Little Leif," he cried. "My old neighbour! How are you? You've grown so tall – has it really been that long?" He drew in close to Leif, tears glistening in his eyes. "The village," he said desperately, now the initial shock had passed. "My wife, my friends – how are they?"

Erskin's mind whirred. It was all beginning to make sense now. "You were one of the offerings," she said, shock making her voice strange to her ears. "One of the sacrifices made by the Lordsson to keep the dragon happy." She looked around. The others crowded closer to get a better look at the children, murmuring. Erskin saw more faces she recognized. More, and more. She stared at them. "You *all* were!"

Even the scientists were there – those who'd come from the mainland to conduct research, and had never been seen again – although they didn't look as unhappy as the others to be there, so perhaps they, at least, were here by choice.

"The dragon never came for us," replied Alrick. "It was all a lie. The Lordsson brought us here instead, to work. He promises our families will have everything they need as long as we do as he says. And if we don't…" Alrick shuddered and looked at his feet. Of course he had brought them here. The offerings weren't lost to the mountain. The Lordsson had been using the people he selected this way the whole time, just as his father must have done before him. Perhaps, once, the yearly sacrifices made to the dragon were sincere – though what became of the others, who knew. But not any more.

Alrick's voice grew urgent, and he grabbed Leif and Erskin roughly. "Get away before he finds out you've been here. You still have a chance if you leave now. Anyone who sees this place or learns the truth about the mountain, he traps here to keep his drell working."

"Too late," came a voice from the tunnel. "I'm here."

The figure of Aleksander Lordsson strode towards them out of the gloom. Even down here, the gold embroidery on his fine clothes gleamed, and his bright eyes shone in the dark.

The man responsible for the drell was right in front of her, and coming closer. The drell workers shrank back. All the hairs on Erskin's arms stood on end, and Scrat hissed.

"What's happened here?" the Lordsson demanded, scowling. "Is the drell damaged?"

Alrick loosened his grip on the children's clothes, but didn't let go. Erskin could hear his breathing quicken. "Yes, but it's nothing we can't fix, sir."

"Good. See that it happens immediately," the Lordsson said, his tone icy.

Alrick nodded and instructed some of the group to start mending the smashed machinery. The luma strands still spilling from the broken wires seemed to bounce off their clothes as they worked. Erskin wondered about the suits they wore – it wasn't a material she'd ever seen, and luma seemed unable to pass through. If it couldn't get in, that would mean it also couldn't get out, so they were clearly protecting the workers from the effects of the drell: preserving whatever power they had, which they could use for the good of the machine. The Lordsson wore something like it too, Erskin noticed – although his was more finely hewn and worn beneath his clothes, visible only at the neck.

The Lordsson turned to the children and studied each of them, one after the other. Erskin and Leif withered under his gaze, and Birgit paled. *"You three,"* he said. "Do you know how much trouble you've caused in the village? Your parents wanted a search party to come up here. On Mountainfell. The idea of it! I can't have people wandering round, disrupting the drelling. And it's far too dangerous. Imagine, risking all this" – he gestured around him – "for some village children. Especially ones so *hex-addled*." He sneered and Erskin flinched. "Yes, I know all about you." He pointed at Leif and Erskin. "Sneaking off. Keeping pets. Upsetting normal village folk."

Erskin gritted her teeth. If someone had said that to her before this whole journey, she might've been overcome with embarrassment and shame. But now she could feel anger fizzing and popping under her skin. Perhaps she and Leif *were* weird, but who cared. They were the only people like them, and that made her proud.

Leif raised his eyebrow at Erskin and they shared a look of scorn. "I don't care what you think of us," Erskin said. "You're destroying Mountainfell and unless you stop using the drell, all the plants and the creatures will die. Don't you get it? We should be protecting Mountainfell and treating it with respect. Not draining it for everything it's worth. It's just pure greed." She glared at the Lordsson's travelling cape made entirely of fur – dappled bronze, white and gold, just like that of the wood foxes she'd run from on the lower slope. Now that she could see him more clearly through the dust and gloom, Erskin noticed that beneath his cape it looked like he was holding something under one arm.

"Greed?" Aleksander scoffed. "Everything I've ever done has been for the village. To make sure we prosper. To make sure we don't starve. It's my responsibility as Lordsson and, one day, as *Lord*, of Lofotby. But what would you know?" He signalled to one of the scientists. "Take them away."

Someone moved forwards – a man Erskin didn't recognize. For a second, he hesitated, glancing back at the Lordsson. But then he grabbed Leif and Erskin. Another person seized Birgit's arm.

"What are you doing?" Erskin cried.

"I'm sorry," muttered Aleksander, "but now you know about the drell you can never go home. I can't have you telling the village what you've seen."

"You can't keep us here!" Erskin yelled over her shoulder as the scientists began marching them away. Her voice echoed down the long, luma-lit tunnel. "And you can't keep taking luma. Please." It made no difference. Aleksander waved them away, and the scientists moved them further down the corridor.

But they had to do something. Luma was still spilling out of parts of the damaged drell and it gave her an idea. She put her hand against one of the broken wires as they passed. Luma strands started to be absorbed by her palm – just enough to give her a little of her power back. Leif saw and did the same, keeping his hand low so no one would notice.

They shared a look of understanding, and Leif began whispering something under his breath. He was talking to the trees.

Scrat, Erskin thought, *get ready to attack...* "Now!" Erskin shouted.

Scrat stood bolt upright on her shoulders. *SCRAT GOOO!* He launched himself at the face of the person holding them, all teeth and claws. At the same time, a tree root slipped round the foot of the person who had Birgit. The children wrenched out of the scientists' hold and ran for it.

"Stop!" Aleksander made a grab for Erskin with his free arm, but she twisted out of his grasp. As she did so Aleksander's fur cape shifted, and she caught a brief glimpse of the thing he was holding on to under there: a sliver of something bright. It was Torkel's egg.

Birgit and Leif tore down the tunnel, but Erskin couldn't leave, not without Torkel's baby. "The dragon's egg! You stole it," she said, rounding on Aleksander.

Scrat, having launched his attack, ran straight back up Erskin's leg and wrapped around her shoulders again, hissing and spitting at the scientists and workers. "You have to give it back," Erskin went on. "It belongs with its parent, not you. The egg's in pain. I've felt it."

Aleksander looked taken aback. "So that's what this is," he muttered to himself. "A dragon's egg. Even more valuable than I thought."

The pounding of Birgit's and Leif's feet had stopped now, and Erskin knew they were coming back to see why she hadn't followed. The egg gleamed white and gold. Occasionally, white mist rolled across its surface, like clouds. It was beautiful.

Torkelchild? Erskin tried projecting her thoughts, but a sharp splitting pain instantly sliced through her head, and she watched golden strands leave her, drawn to the machine. The drell was still draining what little luma she had.

"Torkel's egg... You stole it," accused Leif, coming back to stand by Erskin.

"No," replied Aleksander. "I *found* it. The tremor must have released it through the rock, into my drell site. I dug it out with my own hands. And that makes it mine."

"It doesn't!" cried Erskin.

"You tell him, Erskin," growled Birgit.

"Enough." Aleksander slipped the egg back under his cape and raised a hand. "Take them away. Put them somewhere until we can bring them under control. And, Alrick, fix all this." He gestured at the drell. "It will all need to be repaired properly. At least it's mostly surface damage, nothing serious."

Erskin's heart sank.

"You don't understand," Leif piped up. "The tremors are *caused* by the drell. It's taking too much luma and now the mountain is crumbling. Sibella says that—"

"Did you say Sibella?" the Lordsson asked, cutting Leif off. He swivelled on his heel to look at them. His eyes were wide and his face looked drawn. As if a mask had slipped to show a real person underneath. All the others in the tunnel stopped, and were silent.

The hand that wasn't holding the egg travelled to the golden pin that he always wore on his lapel – his family crest. He rubbed the surface of it absent-mindedly again with his thumb.

Leif bit his lip.

"That's right," said Erskin, seething with anger. "We know the whole story. You spread lies and forced her to come here. You abandoned her."

The Lordsson scowled and his voice rose. "You don't know *anything* about it!"

At that moment the ground beneath their feet shuddered. Erskin felt the rumble travel through her legs. Small, loosened pieces of dust and a smattering of sand-like rock fell from the roof. The realization hit Erskin hard in the gut – it was the start of another tremor.

A giant, roaring rumble came from all around. The whole tunnel shuddered and shook. The drell groaned as the roof split and rocks began to fall. The ground under their feet seemed to rise and tip. The Lordsson staggered back, clutching the egg, as all around came the shouts and screams of the scientists and drell workers. Then came a terrible, metallic wrenching as the drell itself warped.

Scrat screeched and dug in his claws. Erskin fell hard against the wall and managed to grab Leif just before he slipped over onto the floor. They stared at each other with panic in their eyes. Erskin's heart thundered beneath her ribs. What was happening? It felt as if the whole tunnel was collapsing on top of them. Would they be buried down here, with no way to escape?

Birgit dashed over and threw her arms around Erskin and Leif, protecting them from the falling debris. The sudden barrage of stones and dirt stung and cut wherever they hit: exposed necks, arms, the back of heads. Screams echoed through the tunnel until they were all that Erskin could hear.

34

THE RUMBLING AND SHAKING FINALLY STOPPED. Then came shouts and moans. Erskin gasped as Birgit stepped back and she could see the destruction clearly for herself. Light now flooded the cavern, and as the dust cleared Erskin could see why. Half of the cavern had cracked wide open, which let in the light from outside, and broken bits of metallic tubes now dangled everywhere. Golden threads spilled like water out of the open tubes and jagged tears in the machine. People were brushing themselves off and helping others from the rubble. Close by, the Lordsson picked himself up and dusted himself down. There was a large tear in the clothes across his chest and protective suit beneath, but otherwise he seemed unharmed. He still clutched the egg to him.

"Leif," said Erskin. "Listen to that."

Leif frowned, concentrating. "I don't hear anything."

"Exactly." Erskin's eyes grew wide and round. "No machine noise. The drell – I think it's been broken by the tremor."

Aleksander must have realized it too, because he was dashing to and fro between the broken tubes. "No! Not my drell..." The luma swirled around his feet as he moved and caught at his legs – for some reason it seemed to be drawn to him.

A howl came from one of the men in Aleksander's team. It was Alrick. He had clambered across the pile of rubble that now littered the tunnel and was staring out of the collapsed wall through which daylight flooded in.

"What's all this?" asked Aleksander. "Come on. Out with it." He drew the egg tight against his chest and tried to sound calm, but everyone heard the tremble in his voice. Free luma strands were still climbing up Aleksander's body, and now they were drifting towards the egg, like tiny golden moths attracted to light. But Alrick seemed too shaken to form words. Tears were already streaking through the dust on his face. All the hairs on the back of Erskin's neck stood up. Something terrible had happened out there.

Erskin couldn't take it any longer. She had to see. With Scrat around her shoulders, she scrambled up the rubble towards the opening.

Erskin took the first gulps of clean, fresh air that she'd had in hours, but the daylight dazzled her. She couldn't make out anything except shapes. The others began clambering over too. Erskin shielded her eyes and squinted, desperate to see and desperate to keep her balance as the ground rumbled. Finally, the world around her slid into focus.

They were on the village side of the mountain, with a huge sweep of the landscape visible all the way to ground level and out to sea – the village nestled between the mountain and the coast.

That's when Erskin finally understood what she was seeing, and her stomach squeezed so tight that she retched. Part of the weakened mountainside had fallen away, leaving a trail of destruction: a brown-grey gash, as if some giant beast had clawed a terrible, long streak through it. Trees lay strewn, uprooted and broken. But worse than that was the huge overhang that was held to the rest of the mountain by only a few stray tree roots. It could fall at any minute. Nudged by a breeze. Persuaded by gravity.

If that overhang fell away, the entire village would be buried, and everyone in it.

Erskin's whole body felt numb, her throat as dry as the earth that had crumbled away. She couldn't make out what anyone around her was saying yet, except that she was vaguely aware of their horrified cries.

"No," she heard Aleksander say from somewhere close by. "No. I can fix this..."

Anger rolled over Erskin like a tidal wave. "See what you've done, Lordsson. You and your—" But when she looked round, Aleksander wasn't beside her any more. She wheeled round to find him backing away.

The egg in his hands was glowing so brightly now that it hurt her eyes. All around, golden luma, leaking from the drell, was flooding into it – being absorbed, faster and faster. Hadn't Torkel shown her how their egg needed luma to grow, and drew it in? But now it seemed to be mopping up all the luma that the drell had spilled, half a mountain's worth, without letting any go. It was acting almost like the machine. Something was very wrong.

Erskin tried to reach the egg with her mind, but a wall of terror from the creature inside almost knocked her over. At the same time a terrible screaming rang in her ears – like that of a baby hysterical with a fever. It's frightened, Erskin realized. Its luma has been stolen by the drell. It almost died. And now it's absorbing all the luma it can, and it's too scared to let go.

"Lordsson," Erskin said. "Give me the egg. Something's wrong with it. It's just a baby and it needs comfort to put things right. It needs the dragon."

"Lordsson, please, don't be foolish," chimed in Leif, who'd seen the Lordsson edging away from them. "Do what Erskin says – give the egg back."

"You heard them," said Birgit. "Give. It. Back."

Aleksander's face crumpled with panic, and he shook his head wildly. "The egg's all I have left now. I can't give it back. Don't come near me. Don't follow!" As his arm crossed his body, the egg glowed bright, and a barrage of rocks lifted up and flung themselves at Erskin, Leif and Birgit. All three of them ducked as rocks whizzed past their heads. Aleksander stared at his own hand, amazed, and then at the egg. He, too, had begun to glow – an aura of gold hanging around him, rising up from where he held the egg. Where he was touching the egg, luma was being drawn into him, too.

Then he turned and fled. All they could hear was the sound of rocks crashing and grinding as he forced his way through the blocked tunnel, the egg's power at his fingertips.

35

THE MOUNTAINSIDE GROANED LIKE A LIVING creature. Wrapped around Erskin's neck, Scrat let out a terrified yowl. Erskin flung out her hands for balance and found Leif's and Birgit's. The land around them was shifting, sliding...

"We have to stop Aleksander," Erskin said, but her eyes stayed fixed on the overhang of earth and the panicked drell workers. It wasn't only the village that was in danger. If the earth fell, everyone here would fall too.

"Alrick!" Erskin spun round, searching the group until she found him. "Can't you and the others do something? You have powers, don't you?"

Alrick stared back at her, face haggard and shoulders hunched. "For fixing a machine, kid. Not a mountain." A number of the drell workers murmured in agreement. "Our best bet is to get away and pray the villagers are evacuating to the docks," he said. "Let Aleksander go. Who cares about an egg?"

So, they'd given up. Erskin shook her head. No. It wasn't just an egg. And there was still a chance. She was about to reply when Leif interrupted.

"Hey. You there!" Leif bellowed across the mountainside, apparently at nothing. He groaned and began to pace.

Erskin frowned. "What on Yor are you doing?"

"I'm going to talk to the trees." He was breathing quickly. "Perhaps, if I can persuade them to cling on tight enough with their roots, they can hold the loose rocks back. At least for now. This one's terrified." He looked across at a tiny, battered sapling not far from the opening, which he'd just been shouting to. "I need to go to it, to make it listen. You go after the Lordsson." He gave a nervous grimace.

Tears rose in Erskin's eyes at Leif's bravery. She threw her arms around him, and they hugged. "How will you talk to them all? Can you make them all hear you?"

"There's that secret I told you about trees," came his muffled reply from against her. His breath felt hot as it blew through her hair, and Scrat sniffed the top of his head and mewed. "They talk to *each other*. If

I can speak to the sapling, I should be able to speak to them all." He pulled away and grimaced again. "Trust me."

Erskin nodded. "I do."

Birgit eyed them both, taking it all in. Then said, solemnly, "Be careful, Leif."

Leif nodded, and gulped. As the bewildered drell workers stared in horror at the mountainside and others took their first slow, shaky steps across it, away from the landslide, Leif clambered out over the ragged ledge of the mountainside and into the open air. He started to edge his way over the shifting rock to the sapling. "Um. Hi there. Can you hear me? Don't be afraid." The ground underfoot juddered, sending a shower of stones tumbling away. Leif froze, watching them fall. The sapling itself quivered. Leif gritted his teeth and carried on.

Birgit gasped beside Erskin.

Erskin willed him on. Just a few more steps. Two. One more to go.

Finally, the sapling was within Leif's grasp. "It's OK. I'm with you. See?" He stretched out for it over a deep crack in the ground. Frustratingly, agonizingly, it was just out of his reach. Erskin saw his shoulders sag in defeat. But then something changed. The sapling moved. Had the ground shifted again?

No. This was something different. As she watched, the sapling lowered one of its branches until it was touching Leif's palm. Leif and the tree looked just like they were holding hands.

If Erskin hadn't been so afraid of falling, she would've leaped up and down. He'd done it.

As Leif touched the sapling's branch, he closed his eyes and seemed to whisper something to it. The sapling rustled its tiny leaves in response. What followed was a noise like a sudden rush of water – except that's not what it was. It was all the trees for miles around rustling their leaves as though blown in a gale. But Erskin knew what they were really doing was talking to one another.

Tree roots began to twist around the loose rocks in front of them, holding them tight. It was happening everywhere. Even down by the overhang, the nearby trees gripped the ground, weaving around and through it, pushed up from underneath with their branches. Anything to hold a second landslide back.

Erskin let out a small cry of joy. Leif had done it, but then she caught sight of him. His jaw was clenched and he looked worn. Communicating with all the trees like this and holding them all together was an enormous strain on him. He couldn't hold on for ever. But Erskin could still do something. First, she could get the people off this overhang. Then she would go after the egg. She must save Torkel's child, and perhaps she could convince it to put the luma it had absorbed back into the mountain and save the village. It was a long shot, but she had to try.

She closed her eyes and stretched the fingertips of her mind towards Torkel's. She found it quickly – with the drell damaged she finally had some luma back. *Torkel. The drell is broken, and I've found your egg. But we need you.*

A far-off roar came in response. Aleksander's workers wheeled round, searching the skies, and Birgit went white – but Erskin sighed with relief. The shadow of the dragon snaked behind the veil of cloud that separated them – and then it plunged through. Smashed and shattered, the drell could no longer do them harm. The workers scrambled back inside the devastated cavern for safety, but Erskin didn't budge. Sibella was riding on Torkel's back, her dark hair and cloak billowing around her. Her expression was grave.

Torkel wheeled above the shifting ground. One wrong move and they could send everything tumbling... Finally, they touched down and slid, claws digging in to stop themselves. Erskin ran to them, stroking the dragon's iridescent scales.

Where is my child? Torkel spoke in her mind.

Erskin shook her head. "The Lordsson has the egg, and something's wrong, because it's absorbing all the luma and not letting it go. I'm going to make it right, Torkel. You have to trust me, but first please help me get these people to safety before it's too late."

The dragon roared, and the wordless despair and fury of it flooded Erskin's senses. For a moment she couldn't think for herself, or even breathe. It was hard for her to bear the weight of such a big heart as Torkel's. *My egg, stolen,* they lamented. *Our luma, stolen. And now the home I love is destroyed. How could you ask this of me?*

Erskin buried her face in Torkel's mane and stroked their sparkling, scale-flecked jaw. A long, low rumble came from Torkel's throat. *Please,* thought Erskin. *These people don't deserve to die. It's not their fault they're here.*

I will take you, little ones, but no others, came Torkel's thoughts in response. *Many innocent lives will have been lost, and more are yet to die. Many creatures will now be suffering because of the Beast they cared for. I can sense my child again, and they are suffering too, clinging to luma. I must go to them.* The dragon raised its head and roared again with anguish.

"The tunnel's collapsed. I don't think you'll fit

inside, but I'll find your baby. I promise." Erskin hesitated as she tried to push the fog of doubt away. "But please, help us save the humans. People do terrible things, but they're a part of everything too. Just like the creatures and the plants." Erskin could hear the rock beneath them creaking, cracking, groaning. She searched for the mixture of thought and feeling that Torkel had projected into her mind at the edge of the Enchanted Forest, desperate to conjure it with the same power Torkel had, of which the best translation she had was: *Life is precious*. She projected the thought to Torkel.

Torkel breathed a huff of hot air and thought, *Step back*.

Erskin did it with tears in her eyes. Torkel stretched out their long neck.

For a moment Erskin thought they were going to fly off, but then they tipped their head. Erskin's heart swelled. Torkel was going to help them. Sibella swung herself down and teetered on the unstable earth. Unsmiling, and with a second glance at Erskin, she reached out a hand to Alrick. "Come on. Quickly."

"Go ahead," Erskin called out to the workers. "Climb on." The ground was still shifting. Torkel kept having to scramble to stay in one place. The workers looked terrified, some were rooted to the spot, but they had no time to be afraid of the dragon if they wanted to get away from this place – to safety.

Erskin turned to her sister. "You too, Birgit. Go ahead. Torkel won't hurt you again."

Birgit shuddered. "Erskin, no. I can't leave you here! I—"

Erskin flung her arms around her sister and hugged her tight. "There's no time," she said. "You have to go. Trust me, I'll be OK." Besides, they both knew that Birgit was hurt and exhausted. She needed to get home. With tears in her eyes, Birgit allowed Sibella to hoist her onto the dragon's back. Then Erskin passed over Scrat. "Moww!"

"Leif?" Erskin called out to her friend. But Leif shook his head. "No. I'm staying," he said with a grimace. "But, Erskin – you'll have to hurry."

The moment Birgit and the workers were all clinging on, Sibella clambered back up too with Scrat slung round her neck, and Torkel took to the skies.

Good luck, thought Erskin. *And thank you.*

You too, little one, thought Torkel. *Please help my baby. Help Torkelchild put the luma back where it belongs. It's the only way to stop the mountain falling.*

Sibella glanced round to give them one last, fretful look as they snaked off into the distance, towards the safety of the clouds.

The earth shuddered and shook. To Erskin's horror, more cracks spread in front of her eyes, like a giant sprawling root. Further down, the overhang left by the first landslide groaned and shifted even more. At the same time the ground under her feet shunted and rolled. Leif gritted his teeth and the tree roots gripped tighter. Until finally the shaking stopped.

There was no time to waste. Erskin had to get the egg out of Aleksander's hands.

36

MORE ROCKS HAD COLLAPSED IN THE TUNNEL DOWN which Aleksander had fled with the egg, but small holes peppered the heap. The largest was Erskin's size – just about.

Erskin took a deep breath and poked her head inside the gap between the fallen rocks. A cold breeze blew steadily on her face and left her with goosebumps along her arms. That meant it had to lead to the other side – didn't it? With a final glance behind her, she climbed inside the small, dark gap.

Barely any luma light made it into the space where Erskin had crawled, and the jagged sides grew tighter the further in she managed to squeeze. This did not feel good. In fact, it felt very bad. Worse than the hole the trees had made for them.

She took fast, shallow breaths that made her lungs

feel like they were bursting. Erskin's head spun. She knew she was panicking, which was the worst thing she could possibly do in a tight, dark tunnel. But she couldn't help it. She hated being underground.

Something crawled over her hand in the dark, and she shrieked. But it was just a beetle: the type that had healed her and Leif after Sibella poisoned them. She reached into its mind and found it calm. It was happy to be going about its own business. Its peace helped to calm Erskin too. She slowed her breathing down, emptying her lungs fully before taking a slow, deep breath in.

Please could you help me see, little bug? she asked. In response the beetle glowed a vibrant purple. Finally, Erskin could see her surroundings again. And as she crawled deeper, the space got wider. Soon she was able to stand upright. The beetle flashed its goodbye and scuttled off, leaving its purple trail to fade in its wake.

The luma glow beyond was enough to guide Erskin now. She must be almost through the collapsed tunnel. Up ahead, she hoped would be Aleksander and the egg. She *had* to get to the egg. It was ill – suffering – and who knew what it might do with all the luma swirling inside it while in that state?

The air felt charged with luma. It practically

crackled against her skin. It began to feel like the air was resisting her, pushing her back, so that she had to struggle forwards.

She tried to simply keep moving. The tunnel twisted, leading deeper down, until it opened out into a vast chamber. She couldn't help but stare in amazement. Half of it had fallen away in the tremor, so Erskin could see the sweep of devastated mountainside again. What remained looked like a rough version of how she imagined the rooms in Aleksander's grand palatial home. There was a chair at the centre, carved from an ancient tree. A small part of Erskin's brain – the only part of her that wasn't petrified – could admire how beautiful it all was. It must have taken a lot of manpower to make – or a lot of luma magic, she thought, remembering how Aleksander had once used his to build Sibella's cabin, how he'd vowed to use it to improve his father's drell. Perhaps this was also his handiwork. There were painted tiles on the floor, towering, carved stone pillars, and a high-arched ceiling, painted blue with white stars…

That was when Erskin noticed the gaping crack running through the ceiling, and rubble littering the tiles – and it hit her where she'd seen this place before. It was in her visions of the egg. This is where she'd experienced it fall through the earth, and where the Lordsson had found it.

The first violent tremor – on the night before the dragon attacked – must have dislodged the egg from Torkel's nest, sending it tumbling down into this chamber, where the Lordsson had dug it out. That was why Aleksander thought the egg was his – it had practically landed in his lap.

Then the Lordsson's voice resounded. "There you are."

Erskin couldn't see Aleksander anywhere – the whole chamber was littered with large rocks that had fallen in the recent tremors, and they hid parts of the space from view, creating secret corridors and corners that were perfect for hiding in.

He spoke again. "You think you can just walk in and take my egg?" Then came bitter laughter. It echoed all around Erskin and made her feel small. "I told you, it belongs to me now." Aleksander didn't sound like himself at all – perhaps the effect of the tremor and the loss of his precious drell had affected him. Or maybe all that luma energy spilling into him from the egg, along with the baby's fear, was working on him in much darker and more frightening ways.

A surge of luma energy, like a blast of wind, pulsed through the tunnel so that Erskin had to shield her face. The tunnel shook and dust crumbled from above.

"You have to stop this, Aleksander," Erskin called out. "It's not safe here. The egg needs help. It needs its parent. This whole place could collapse at any moment. Mountainfell is sick. Just give me the egg and we can fix this."

"You can't trick me into giving it up," came Aleksander's reply. He sounded even stranger. Who knew what he might do in this state? "I found the egg – it's *mine*."

Fear tightened Erskin's throat. "Lordsson, *please*."

The Lordsson only laughed. "Luma is worth a fortune, and the egg is all I have left now the drell is destroyed."

"If you don't care about the mountain, think about the village," cried Erskin. "The people are trusting you to keep them safe."

The Lordsson laughed again. "With all the luma inside this egg I could rebuild a hundred Lofotbys," he replied.

Erskin edged further into the chamber. There was still no sign of Aleksander – or of the egg. But she had to be careful. Aleksander could be anywhere, and he was dangerous. If she could persuade him to come out of hiding, perhaps she could snatch the egg from him…

"The egg is too powerful for you," said Erskin, walking slowly around the chamber, looking in all the dark corners. "You're making everything worse."

"You sound just like my father," came Aleksander's reply, but his voice could have come from anywhere, given the way the chamber made sound echo. "He's never believed I could handle the power that came with being Lord one day. Always criticizing me for every little mistake. Always calling me weak. But when he sees my prize and how powerful it makes me, he will finally be proud, I know it."

My prize.

This was useless. Aleksander wasn't going to listen to her, and Erskin was running out of time. She needed to try and speak to the egg again. Last time the egg's distress had nearly bowled her over. But she had no choice.

Erskin pressed her body flat against a tall, thin rock shaped like an arrowhead, and braced herself. Carefully she stretched the fingers of her mind into the dimness around her. *Torkelchild,* she thought. *It's OK. I'm here to take you home.* Her words hit a wall of fear and panic so overwhelming that for an instant she couldn't move. She tried to tell herself those were the feelings of the creature inside the egg, and not her own, to ease her limbs into working again.

Focus, she told herself.

She felt around in the darkness with her mind again, prompting and probing. Searching. The wall of panic hit her once more, but this time she gritted her teeth, determined to push through. She led her mind around the wall of it, nudging to find a weak spot.

Until finally, something nudged her back.

The creature growing inside the egg. It was hard to understand its energy behind the shell and the wall of luma static. Its words – if there were any – were just a fuzz. A murmur. Impossible to interpret. But what if she tried images? Would they be stronger? She had to find something that would help the creature trust her.

"You can't hide from me," came Aleksander's voice, breaking her concentration. "I'll find you."

Erskin forced herself to push the sound of his voice away. The air began to crackle. A hum of power grew louder. The egg's luma magic, building again. The hum of it closed in around Erskin, travelled through the ground and up her legs. She covered her ears and glanced around wildly.

I don't know if you can understand me, Torkelchild. But I need your help. We all do. Please. Help!

She turned, sensing a presence behind her – and she was face to face with Aleksander in the flesh. He looked haggard and ill, his clothes torn. The golden family crest pin he always wore on his lapel was smeared with dirt. He stood tall and proud though, in his majestic fur cape, chin raised. And he held the egg. Its luma-light danced in his eyes like lots of little fires. Aleksander's gaze was fixed on it. "So beautiful," he said. "So powerful..."

In Erskin's mind, the child inside the egg screamed. She fell backwards in shock, and, too late, heard the tumbling rocks. Too late, she saw the shadows from the corner of her eye move as the rocks began to topple down upon her. "No," she cried. "Torkelchild, stop! I'm here to help you."

With every last bit of her strength, Erskin poured her memories into the egg. Using all her might, Erskin conjured images from the depths of her mind. The mountain. The cottage on the wall: her home. The Enchanted Forest and the caves, the Creeping Marsh and Sibella's house, airfisk and burrowing birds and lissenynx and glowing beetles and—

And Torkel. Torkel roaring, searching the mountain for their precious egg.

I'm here to take you back to your parent, Torkelchild, Erskin thought. *I want to help you. Please let me.*

The impact never came.

When Erskin opened her eyes, the tumbling rocks were where they had been: hanging in the air, frozen.

Ampa?

Erskin had done it. She had made the connection with the creature inside the egg: Torkelchild.

Your Ampa is near by, Erskin said, remembering that word meant parent. *They're waiting for you.*

37

Everything shook. From beyond the cavern came the sound of groaning, splintering wood – and a boy's cry: Leif's. Both he and the trees were losing their grip. At the same time, Erskin felt Torkelchild turn away from her, its fear building again as the mountain collapsed around them. The rocks it had held aloft crashed to the ground, narrowly missing her. Aleksander cried out. Erskin *had* to do something – to somehow get the luma from that egg. Mountainfell needed it.

The Lordsson staggered and put his hand against a nearby stone for support. He was still staring at the egg, which was glowing now like a small sun in his hands. Luma threads were tangling around him too, knotting up, their light giving him a sickly pallor.

Erskin frowned. "The egg is too powerful, and

it's scared. You need to let it go. I'm afraid it might hurt you." She could feel the baby's fear and panic. "It needs to be with its parent. You have to give it to me so that I can return it. And we have to do it before this whole place collapses."

"Nonsense. No one in their right mind gives up power once they have it. I'd be a fool to give you the egg."

The ground shook, and slabs of rock pulled away from the chamber wall far behind him. Cracks of light shone through. More of the chamber fell away. The pair staggered and the egg almost slipped from Aleksander's hands, but he clutched it tighter to his chest. Erskin felt another surge of fear from the egg. Terror squeezed her throat, but she stood firm. "Please," she shouted, holding out her hands. "Pass it to me."

"Never! Lofotby is my responsibility," he said. "I'm … protecting it."

Once more the ground rumbled and tilted – more violently than before. Erskin was thrown to the floor and so was Aleksander. As he fell, he let go of the egg.

Erskin watched with horror as it tumbled out of his grasp. With all her energy, she threw herself towards it – catching it, just before it smashed onto the hard floor. Her heart pounded in her chest as the hand touching the egg, and then her arm, went numb and began to ache. There was so much power, trapped inside ... too much power ... taken from the broken drell. It needed to be released. She could feel it like a knotted ball of force.

Erskin closed her eyes and tried to make contact with the creature inside again. Aleksander had curled into a ball, clutching his leg. He must have hurt it as he fell. Erskin pushed the sight of him away, reaching out to Torkelchild, but her mind bounced back against the wall of fear and luma static. The egg's memories of its fall through the mountain seared into her brain and its panic overwhelmed her.

Images flashed in front of her eyes. Human hands digging it out, grabbing it, after its fall. And, before that, different hands taking it from its nest, dropping it into the darkness... Erskin frowned. That couldn't be right. It had to be confused. The egg fell through a crack all on its own. But it was clear that human hands – even her own, holding it now – frightened it, reminded it of being separated from Torkel.

She rested it on the ground instead, squeezed her eyes shut and tried to reach out to it again. She'd done this before. She knew Torkelchild was there ... behind all that luma and dread. If only she could reach it.

Torkelchild.

Beside her, Aleksander was quietly whimpering.

She summoned the image of Torkel in her mind – Torkel, its loving parent, who would do anything to protect it. Torkel, the dragon of the mountain. *Torkel, Torkel, Torkel.*

Erskin sharpened her thoughts into an arrow and pushed. Torkelchild responded in a big way. Suddenly it was as if she'd fallen into another realm.

38

ERSKIN SAW HERSELF AS IF FROM ABOVE: A TINY figure battling through a wall of jagged, glowing brightness. It was like one of the visions that the egg had given her. Except this time she was wide awake, and it all felt so real. Somehow Torkelchild had drawn her into the tumult of its mind. And it was as if the power of the vision had temporarily blasted her out of herself.

Every step forward was a struggle, as though she were fighting against a gale, a blizzard. But she had to keep going; had to keep fighting. She mustn't be blown off course.

Torkelchild!

The little figure of herself drove onward. Her viewpoint lowered until she was looking through the eyes of this other version of herself. She pulled and scratched against the wall of bright light, which was like the curve of a sun, but it kept folding back over itself. Pushing her out. She couldn't give up. Leif, her friend, was out there on the mountainside. All those lives in the village – on the mountain – were hanging in the balance...

She pushed forward again with her arms outstretched, determined – and caught hold of something. *Torkelchild.*

Through the overwhelming hiss of static, another noise formed – quiet at first, growing louder. A steady, pulsing sound. A heartbeat.

"You're here," Erskin said. "I can feel you. Show yourself, Torkelchild. I need your help to save the village and the mountain. But we have to do this together. You have to help me."

From behind the bright light, a dark shape swam into view. That was when Erskin saw it properly.

A dragon, just like Torkel – but a deep, smoky grey. Beautiful. It mewled at her and rubbed its feathery mane against her face. Erskin nuzzled into it. This must be what Torkelchild looked like, inside the egg. She was inside the baby's vision, and yet she could feel everything. The softness of the dragon's mane. The slippery-smooth, almost fish-like feel of its scales that were cool and warm at the same time.

The strength of the energy around them, like knotted steel ropes, constantly trying to drive them apart, like a repelling magnet.

"Help me put things right, Torkelchild," said Erskin.

Torkelchild shivered and mewled – it was still afraid.

"It's OK," said Erskin, trying to speak with her feelings as much as words. "I'm afraid too. See? But the drell is broken now, it can't hurt you any more. You have to let the luma go now, or everything around us will die. Trust me. I'll keep you safe."

Torkelchild made a rumbling sound in its nose, lowered its head and licked her eyes, making Erskin jump. *Close your eyes,* it seemed to be telling her. *The luma will be too bright.*

Erskin nodded. She cried out to Aleksander, who was somewhere beyond this vision, in the cave. "Lordsson," she said, "look away. The luma will be too much for you." Who knew if he could hear her though.

She could feel the power building, until it was too much to contain...

She slammed her eyes shut.

Erskin was thrown backwards by the blast. Behind her tightly shut eyes, all she could see was white.

"Mowww?" She was on the ground, and a soft furry face was nuzzling hers. *Wake up, best human. Get off floor.*

When she opened her eyes, Scrat stared back. "Moww!" *You alive – me happy!*

Erskin stared, confused. Everything hurt. "I thought you went with Sibella?" she said, rubbing her forehead.

"He did," came Sibella's voice, and then the witch was standing over her, hands on her hips. Sibella helped her up, and Scrat clambered onto Erskin's shoulders.

"How—"

"I made Torkel set me down. I couldn't let you do this alone. Not after..." But she didn't finish. "You didn't need me, though. You've achieved what I couldn't, Erskin," she said instead, drawing her close. "It really was you who had what it took to heal the mountain. Let me look at you." Sibella grabbed her face, and tears of gratitude swam in her eyes.

Erskin swayed woozily. Her head ached, but after a moment, the dizziness cleared, and Erskin could finally focus again. There was a point of brilliant light on the ground beside them that she couldn't look at directly: the egg. Waves of light gushed from it like a waterfall, flowing out into the open air. It was as if she were standing next to a small sun – but one that had ruptured.

Erskin guessed it was all the trapped luma streaming out of the egg. It had to be.

The light flowed for a long time, leaking between the boulders and the cracks of the cave as it seeped back into the mountain. Erskin, Scrat and Sibella watched it. The trees holding back the landslide burgeoned, their roots thickened and grew strong. Grass and moss wove a carpet over it all. All across the mountain, the waterfall of light left luma-streaked soil, a lush weave of plant life.

But as the light from the egg finally faded away, Erskin remembered Aleksander. When Erskin swivelled round she saw that he was sprawled across the ground, unmoving.

39

Erskin and Sibella hurried over to Aleksander. Erskin felt a pang of guilt that they hadn't noticed him before, but the sight of what was happening on the mountain had been too absorbing.

"Aleksander Lordsson." Sibella knelt towards the collapsed figure, then said in little more than a whisper, "Do you remember an old friend?"

Aleksander groaned. He was still alive.

"Sibella?" Aleksander said. "Is it really you?" His voice was different, softer.

Sibella laughed. "Of course it's me. Do I look like a ghost?"

"Oh, Sibella," said the Lordsson, bowing his head. "I've been so foolish."

Sibella dropped her own head. "Haven't we all?" she murmured.

And the egg's memory of the hands – human hands – scooping it out of its nest and dropping it into darkness came into Erskin's mind. She stared at Sibella. At her hands.

"It was you, wasn't it?" Erskin's voice resounded around the cavern. She was trembling. "Sibella, you dropped the egg through the cracks the tremor had made."

Sibella turned to face Erskin, and her face was filled with sorrow. "Yes."

"I don't understand," gasped Erskin. "Why would you do such a thing?"

"To save the mountain," she answered simply. "I knew that it would die unless I did something. And Torkel wouldn't help, so ... I tricked them. I took their baby away, to force them to see that the villagers were bad. That something had to be done about the drell. And, if I'm honest" – she glanced at Aleksander – "I wanted to *show* the village too. To punish it for everything it had done. To the mountain, and ... to me."

Quietly, Sibella added, "I'll regret it until the end of my days, child. I know my dear friend Torkel will never forgive me for what I've done. I only wanted to hide the egg, for as long as it would take, and conceal its thoughts from the dragon with a spell. But in the tremor the egg slipped from my grasp. I hadn't meant for it to fall into the drell, or to be hurt, or even to be found. If it wasn't for you..." Her voice cracked, and a tear ran down her cheek.

Erskin stared. After everything she'd heard, everything she'd been through, she felt numb. "I'm taking the egg, and I'm calling Torkel to take us away. Now. You two deserve each other." She turned her back on the pair and reached out her hands towards the egg.

May I? she thought to Torkelchild, holding out her hands. But the egg didn't reply. Erskin frowned. *Torkelchild?*

Erskin felt icy coldness climb up her spine. She reached out and touched the egg. No response this time – not even fear. Only the weakest of heartbeats, fading fast. The last wisps of luma drifted away from the egg as its glow began to dim.

"Torkelchild. No!" A sob shuddered out of Erskin.

"What is it? What's happened?" Sibella cried as Erskin clutched the egg to her chest and gasped for breath.

"I think ... I think Torkelchild is dying."

The egg had spent days away from its parent, being hurt by the drell, and had then been overrun with luma – too much for it to handle. The whole ordeal must have been too much for Torkel's egg. It was just a baby, after all. Tears streaked down Erskin's face. She'd promised Torkelchild it would be OK, that she would keep it safe. She'd failed, and it was dying. Not even Erskin's healing powers could help the egg now.

Sibella stared at the egg and turned pale. Then her jaw tightened. "I've stolen enough from Mountainfell. It's time I gave it something of myself." Sibella reached to her chest and began to draw out a long, golden string – the brightest luma Erskin had ever seen.

Aleksander watched her for a moment, then put his hand on her arm. "Here," he said, opening his cape to reveal the torn clothes beneath, "take mine too." The two exchanged a look. And then Sibella pulled another string from Aleksander's chest.

Erskin blinked in amazement and fear. "Sibella?" she said with uncertainty. But the Witch of the Mountain wasn't listening. Her hand entwined with Aleksander's, she pushed the two threads towards the egg, which absorbed them and once again began to glow. In Erskin's mind, Torkelchild's weak pulse grew in strength, until it became a pounding heartbeat once more.

"You saved it," cried Erskin, staring at Sibella. "You saved Torkelchild!"

A weak smile crossed Sibella's lips, before she closed her eyes and fell with Aleksander, collapsing to the ground.

40

ONE MONTH LATER.

It was not yet dayspring when Erskin slipped from the cottage and made her way along the wall by the light of a glow lamp to where she would meet the dragon. Torkel had been in contact this past week – the merest whisper of their thoughts coming from the clouds. At first she'd barely noticed, being so distant. But then Torkelchild had been sending her dreams, too, long before that, so part of her already knew: something exciting was going to happen. The egg was preparing to hatch.

Her sister, Birgit, followed behind, carrying blankets. They were for sitting on, and in case they got too cold, though Erskin had the warmth of Scrat – her living scarf – draped around her neck, whisking his tail. Still, Birgit insisted she bring them just in case, and Erskin didn't mind. She knew her sister liked to be prepared.

Together, they wove their way beside the winding wall that separated the village from Mountainfell, until they came to a huge gap. This part had been destroyed in the terrible landslide. Not that long ago, the Lordsson would have had the wall rebuilt immediately – higher, and stronger, to keep people away from Mountainfell, but mostly to hide his family's secret: the drell. Not now.

The Lordsson was gone, and the villagers no longer feared the mountain. Not after it had turned out that its most dreaded beast – the cloud dragon – was no flesh-eater after all. And especially since the dragon had brought home all their missing loved ones on their back. These days green moss grew over the collapsed parts of the wall and white flowers of remembering sprouted through the gaps. Erskin and Birgit crossed through into a field where a few trees grew. That was where they joined Leif.

He beamed up at them and straight away started to chat as Birgit and Erskin lay down their blankets and settled beside him. Erskin listened, smiling, while she stroked Scrattletak – or Fluffkins, as he was sometimes known – and a purr vibrated through his rounded, furry tummy. Occasionally the trees would rustle, and Leif would tell them what they'd said.

In Erskin's pocket, a cob mouse woke from its warm curl of sleep. It felt a pang of hunger that nudged at Erskin's mind. She passed it a crumb and felt tiny, gentle paws pull it from her fingers.

Since the landslide she'd kept her promise to Torkel and had used her luma to heal the creatures who could be healed. Most of them she had healed on the mountain, and that was where they had stayed – they were wild, after all. But some, like the cob mouse, stayed with her in the cottage (kept safe, of course, from the jaws of Scrat) until they were well enough to leave. Her parents had objected at first, but they had soon grown used to it, and now they even liked to help. Feeding the uni-horned deer was her mam's favourite job, and her dad enjoyed the company of the tellerhawks.

They hadn't seen the dragon since that day on the mountain when Aleksander and Sibella had sacrificed themselves to save the egg. It was a dragon's way to be reclusive, after all, and Torkel's home was at the summit, where they mostly liked to stay. Erskin had told Torkel everything – about the terrible thing Sibella had done, but also how she'd given her life for Torkelchild. Torkel had kept their thoughts on it all private, but Erskin knew that they were a forgiving creature at heart. And they had been friends with Sibella once.

Since the village had learned the truth about the drelling from those workers who had returned, they'd grown angry, and rounded on the palace to demand answers from the Lord. But he was nowhere to be found. Having seen the dragon bring back all those who'd been kept in the drell and realized the truth was out, he must have secretly slipped away – likely paying for passage aboard a trade ship. The scientists from the mainland, too, had quickly disappeared during the commotion of the workers' return – perhaps on the same boat as the Lord. He hadn't even waited to hear news about his son.

In the Lord's absence, a small council of villagers had cobbled themselves together while the people of Lofotby figured out what to do. It was decided that Erskin's father should still be the Mountain Keeper, but that his job should change. He no longer patrolled the wall to warn of danger from the mountain. Instead, it was her father's duty to protect Mountainfell, to watch over it and to make sure all of nature stayed in balance. He wanted to make sure that no one ever tried to steal its luma again. His was now the most respected role in all of Lofotby.

Everyone who'd been involved in saving the village – and the mountain – from disaster had been honoured by the new council. The ceremony had been held in the village square where the market usually stood, but that day there was only a small platform – and a lot of people. Erskin could remember the ceremony as if it had only just happened, and how scared she'd been in front of all those people. "You have ridden a dragon, Erskin," her father had reminded her, with a wry smile. "You can't possibly be scared of a little crowd like this." He'd wrapped up Erskin and Birgit in his blanket-like hug. The thing was it wasn't such a little crowd. It was a big crowd. All the villagers, and all the traders in the bay that day, had attended.

One by one, they had each been called forward to be given their titles by the council. Erskin, the Mountain Keeper in Waiting, guided of course by her Mountain Keeper father, Lorens. Leif was the Tree Keeper, and Birgit became the Hark Maiden, for her skill at sensing and warning of danger.

Tonight, however, it was just them, waiting for the dragon in silence but for Scrat's rumbling purr, their faces turned to Mountainfell. Through Scrat's fur, Erskin felt a flicker of interest, a subtle tensing of his body that told her someone was coming. He hopped down from her shoulders and began to pace in front of them. "Prrow."

Sometimes she wondered about Scrat. He was such an enigma. No one really knew where he was from, or why he'd chosen to come to Erskin. She'd thought about their whole adventure a lot, this last month, and how Scrat had been with her at almost every turn, as if subtly guiding her.

The mountain knows what it needs and usually finds a way to get it, Sibella had once told them.

You wouldn't know anything about that, would you, Scrat? Erskin asked him now in her mind, recalling the conversation.

Scrat simply licked a paw, but the silver markings on his chest shifted into the shape of a triangle – or, possibly, a mountain. Stunned at first, Erskin quickly shook her head and laughed it off, smiling at Leif and Birgit as they stared at her, puzzled. Scrat, her loveable, daft cat, some sort of agent of the mountain? No. Surely not.

As they watched, what looked like a sliver of mist broke away from the mountaintop and wove its way down towards them. It was what they had all been waiting for.

The wisp of mist weaved patterns in the air and grew closer – and larger – and it was clear it wasn't mist, or cloud, but Torkel, gleaming in the moonlight. The dragon landed in front of them lightly, barely shaking the ground. Scrat sat up, ears pricked.

"Torkel!" Erskin ran over and buried her head in their mane.

It is good to see you, little one, thought Torkel. *All of you.*

Erskin turned back to Birgit and Leif. "Are you ready?" she asked them.

Leif nodded, his eyes bright, but Birgit looked less sure. "As I'll ever be," she murmured, but she gave Erskin a wink and a smile. It didn't matter if they were ready or not. Erskin's dreams of the egg had been getting gradually more powerful, until Torkel finally placed the thought in her mind that it was time. If they didn't want to miss the hatching, it was now or never.

No sooner had they clambered onto Torkel's back than they set off, twisting up into the sky. Everything fell away from them, the field, the wall, the village. Lofotby's lights twinkled like stars.

The air at the summit was different. Thinner, with a strange, smoky scent. Torkel brought them down inside a large, hollowed-out dip: a shelter from the wind and elements. Beyond and below, the permanent clouds looked like snowy lands, floating untethered from the earth.

Erskin, Leif and Birgit slipped down from Torkel's neck. The dragon rested in a ring shape around them. At the very centre of the hollow sat the egg, a large crack that gleamed gold running across its surface. And, as they waited, more cracks spread out from it.

Deep in their throat, Torkel purred. *My child wanted you to be here,* they thought and turned their dark eyes towards Erskin. *After everything that happened, they are connected to you now.*

Erskin beamed so hard that tears rolled down her cheeks. "We wouldn't have missed this for anything."

"Totally, what Erskin said," Leif added, picking up on the conversation. "It's an honour to watch a dragon hatch." For once, he'd run out of words and gripped one of Sibella's books tight to his chest – along with a pen.

Birgit smiled, her eyes glassy with wonder.

Soon, cracks covered the entire surface of the egg. The golden light spread, until it hurt to look at it. Then the eggshell burned away into glittering vapour and dust. And there they were: Torkelchild, just as they had appeared in Erskin's vision.

Torkelchild mewed. *Ampa?*

My baby. Torkel drew their face close and Torkelchild nuzzled them and yipped with pleasure. Torkelchild slithered through the air towards the children, wrapping themselves around each of them, before returning to their *ampa*.

The intensity of it was all too much for Erskin. With one hand buried in Scrat's fur, she backed away and plucked a flower of remembering, growing at the side of Torkel's shelter. Holding it to her heart, she fixed this memory – and all the wonderful things that had happened since the village and the mountain was saved – deep inside it.

They all watched as Torkel and their child took to the air. There they rolled and dived with one another, twisting through the clouds around Mountainfell.

Spirits' Waterfall

FEW ALIVE HAVE SEEN THIS PLACE. MOST DON'T even know it exists. They think it's a frightening fable. Even if they did believe, they'd still have to charm their way past the trees that keep its secrets. Sibella and Aleksander are there, and they are happy, because they're together.

Sibella spends her days mesmerized by the cool, clear pool where the waterfall sings and makes ripples and whorls, as the pebbles at the bottom gleam like gems. There are animals here, and birds and fish. All are different. All are beautiful. There are also plants and flowers and vegetables and roots that she has never seen before. In fact, there's always something new to explore. She likes to observe their magical properties by touching the luma of each thing she sees. Already she's learned so much. And so has Aleksander. Somehow he's also kept a little magic, which he uses to create dens for animals, nests for birds.

There are always donderline seeds here, too. Sibella has no idea where they come from, or how they get here. But there are always so many that at times the grass at the pool's edge looks as though it's peppered with snow.

Sibella thinks they could stay here for eternity and there would always be something new to explore. But they are fading. Soon, Sibella knows, their time lingering at the water's edge will be over. But they aren't afraid. Their energy will go back to the mountain, helping it to thrive. And they will be together.

Every day here is much the same as the last. Each blends into the next. But today, something is different. Sibella hears a noise. It can't be, but it sounds a little like footsteps. And whispers.

"... leave it there. That's right. Perfect."

"... still not sure why you're doing this, Erskin."

"Birgit, I want them to know how they helped in the end. That what they did was... Leif, tell the trees..."

Sibella and Aleksander drift closer to the sound. The leaves of the trees rustle, and their trunks begin to creak. As the pair watch, the trees part. No one is there on the other side, but on the ground is a small offering, white and gleaming.

A plucked flower of remembering, just for them.

Acknowledgements

The problem is that I'd like to thank everyone – but that would take more space than the story. I just want to let you know that, whether you're a reader, writer, reviewer, bookseller, blogger, friend, family member (or all or none of the above), your support has meant everything, and I'm grateful to you from the bottom of my heart.

This includes my agent, Bryony of DKW Literary Agency and everyone at Walker Books, especially my editor, Annalie, and Ben and Sandra for producing another spectacular cover. Thanks too to all the friends who've kept me going, who root for me and continue to put up with me: you're the absolute best. That's counting the brilliant new DKW-crew friends I've met via our online writer chats (that steer more towards octopuses, time loops, Star Wars and piranha-wrangling than writing, and which I love all the more for that).

Which leads me to how incredibly kind and generous so many writers are with their time, author quotes, reviews and general support: thank you, all, for that – I hope you know that you do more than just offer a kindness, you help to restore a little of my faith in humanity. The same goes for you all: really, those glimmers of kindness matter, so whatever and whoever they're directed at, keep putting them out into the world. Thank you as well to the Society of Authors for practical help, and Ece with her "Letters from Now", which have given me sustenance this year.

A special shout-out goes to my parents Lisa and Simon, and the rest of my family – the Ortons, Axons, Pullaras, Wildings and all associated clans. Again, your support is invaluable. Matt and Isaac, you two are the joy of my life.

Finally I'd like to thank you, the person reading this. Keep reading, keep being you, and always stay weird. Those who don't conform are the ones who change the world.